A Home Subscription! It's the easiest and most convenient way to get every one of the exciting Coventry Romance Novels! ...And you get 4 of them FREE!

You pay nothing extra for this convenience: there are no additional charges...you don't even pay for postage! Fill out and send us the handy coupon now, and we'll send you 4 exciting Coventry Romance novels absolutely FREE!

SEND NO MONEY, GET THESE
FOUR BOOKS
FREE!

- -

CO881

MAIL THIS COUPON TODAY TO:
COVENTRY HOME
SUBSCRIPTION SERVICE
6 COMMERCIAL STREET
HICKSVILLE, NEW YORK 11801

YES, please start a Coventry Romance Home Subscription in my name, and send me FREE and without obligation to buy, my 4 Coventry Romances. If you do not hear from me after I have examined my 4 FREE books, please send me the 6 new Coventry Romances each month as soon as they come off the presses. I understand that I will be billed only $9.00 for all 6 books. There are no shipping and handling nor any other hidden charges. There is no minimum number of monthly purchases that I have to make. In fact, I can cancel my subscription at any time. The first 4 FREE books are mine to keep as a gift, even if I do not buy any additional books.

For added convenience, your monthly subscription may be charged automatically to your credit card.

☐ Master Charge   ☐ Visa
    42101   **42101**

Credit Card # _____

Expiration Date_____

Name_____
                           (Please Print)

Address_____

City_____State_____Zip _____

Signature_____

☐ Bill Me Direct Each Month **40105**

Prices subject to change without notice.
Publisher reserves the right to substitute alternate FREE books. Sales tax collected where required by law. Offer valid for new members only.

DANCE
FOR A LADY

Eileen Jackson

FAWCETT COVENTRY • NEW YORK

DANCE FOR A LADY

Published by Fawcett Coventry Books, a unit of CBS Publications, the Consumer Publishing Division of CBS Inc.

Copyright © 1981 by Eileen Jackson

ISBN: 0-449-50201-5

Printed in the United States of America

First Fawcett Coventry printing: August 1981

10 9 8 7 6 5 4 3 2 1

One

THE FAIR CITY OF BATH was visible from Tog Hill on a clear day, but this morning it was shrouded by the misty rain which was swiftly deteriorating into a steady downpour.

Anabel toiled up the hill, her half boots sinking into muddy potholes, her gown giving her increasing weight to carry as the hem became soaked. Water blew under the hood of her cloak and trickled in chill rivulets down her neck and slender back.

A less restrained woman might have cursed the ill luck which had marred her flight, but long years of suppression had gifted Anabel with the resignation to force her legs along in silent resolve.

There seemed something malevolent in a fate which permitted her aunt to wake early with a headache when usually she slept till well after eight o'clock. Anabel had been disturbed by Tabitha, her aunt's maid, and asked—no, commanded—recalled Anabel as she visualized the maid's insolent face, to attend her aunt and administer soothing massage.

It had been over an hour before she had been

released, her aunt scarcely troubling to render thanks, and Anabel had raced to her bedchamber, thrown on her cloak, grabbed her bundle and her precious box and hurried out through a small side door.

She arrived at the main road from Wick in Gloucestershire to London in time to see the departing back of the stagecoach.

She shouted and ran in a futile effort to stop the coach, but her voice was drowned by the clatter of wheels on the stony road and the thunder of hooves as the horses were whipped to a speed which might take them at least part way up Tog Hill before the outside passengers were forced to disembark and walk.

Almost succumbing to tears of frustration, Anabel sat upon a milestone and waited for her heart to stop its frantic beat. Not for a moment did she consider returning to Harcourt Manor. Tonight was to be the occasion of a party during which her betrothal to her cousin, Miles Bulmore, was to be announced. In spite of her vulnerable position Anabel managed a grim smile at the thought of the consternation her note would cause in her uncle's household. From the age of eight she had been taught that her destiny was to wed the only son of the Bulmore family and now everyone professed to believe that the choice was hers also.

Her protests, begun at the age of fourteen, were voiced in the undemonstrative tones she had learned were best. They were disregarded. When she continued her gentle insistence, her aunt and uncle reminded her coldly that they had been generous enough to give her shelter and rear her with their own children.

Experience had taught Anabel that opposition led to a deterioration in her already unquiet life, but desperation kept her firm in her rejection of Miles.

Her reasons, she knew, would be regarded with contemptuous disbelief so she did not voice her opinion of Miles. Outwardly compliant, inwardly stubborn, she made secret vows that nothing would ever induce her to enter the close bonds of matrimony with a man she despised.

At nineteen he was a year younger than Anabel and memories of their nursery days permeated her life. His hair-pulling, his tricks pursued to the bounds of cruelty, his tantrums when she would not obey him, his taunts at her lack of beauty had scarred her.

In the end her unwavering refusal to regard Miles as a suitor impressed the family for she was told in a falsely jocular manner by her uncle that it was time to stop showing such maidenly reserve and accept her good fortune in a sensible way.

Anabel, so long at the mercy of her mercenary and unimaginative relatives, knew that her strength of will had been eroded. If once they achieved their purpose and announced her be-trothal publicly she was sure she would never find the resolve to defy convention in the face of local society. So she took what secretly she considered a cowardly way out of her dilemma. She fled and meant to remain hidden until she was safe. Miles would never have the power over her which marriage would bestow. Her shudder turned to a shiver as she realized that it was spitting with icy rain and she was growing cold; she picked up her belongings and began to walk in the direction of London with rigid determination.

She had never been farther from home than Bath, and once, Bristol, long ago when Mama and Papa were alive, but everyone knew that London was the place to seek a living and that she was resolved to do. When she arrived at an inn she would wait for a coach.

At the top of the hill she paused for breath and leaned on a low stone wall. She wished she had eaten, but her aunt's summons had made it impossible to wait for food. She had intended to bring provisions, but all she had grabbed in her hasty rush was an apple which now she chewed slowly, trying to make it last. Her appetite was not large, but exercise had sharpened it and she pushed back the memory of the food-laden table at the manor.

Independence first, she assured herself. Food later! She would repine no more over her spoiled plans but press on and tackle problems as they arose.

As she bent to pick up her bundle she heard the sound of approaching hooves and made a quick move toward a low-hanging clump of trees. If one of the local folk should be abroad she would surely be apprehended. Everyone knew of her uncle's plans for her and, as a magistrate, he held power and influence.

Once more the haste with which she had escaped made itself apparent. She had not stopped to reinforce the faulty catch of her box with a cord. It sprang open and the contents spilled out onto the filthy wet road. Anabel gave a cry of anguish as her precious stock in trade rolled about in pools and mud and as the carriage drew nearer she leaped forward and fell to her knees almost beneath the horses' iron-shod hooves. The startled postilions reined in so hard that the leading pair reared, dragging the wheelers sideways. The light post chaise swayed dangerously, teetered on two wheels for an instant, then landed with a bone-jarring crunch, back on four wheels.

"God damn you to hell!" The voice came from within the coach and the postilions glared down at Anabel, mouthing their fury. She scarcely heard them as she crouched picking up charcoal and wiping it before replacing it in her box. Pencils, pots of paint and unmixed powder colors still thankfully sealed in oilcoth were all retrieved and finally Anabel stood. Her viewpoint led her to look straight through the coach window into the face of a man who was registering contemptuous rage.

"How dare you, woman! You might have maimed one of my horses!"

Anabel's fury rose to match his, but she managed a small ironical curtsey. "I should never want to be the means of injuring an animal, sir, but I had to save my possessions."

His eyes were veiled slits as he replied, "Damn your possessions! What can a few bits of trumpery rubbish carried by a serving wench matter compared with my prime bits of blood and bone?"

Anabel gave him back his stare. "A serving

wench's treasures may never compare with anything you own, sir, but to her they have infinitely more value, being all she has in the world."

The carriage door was flung open and the man jumped lightly down. Anabel stared at him. She had recognized him at once as the late visitor to her uncle's household and she felt inward-burning shame. He had been inveigled to Harcourt Manor in the hope that her cousin, Drusilla, would find a way to compromise him into marriage. The scheme had failed and Paul, Viscount Ryder, had left yesterday in a mood which did not appear to have improved during his overnight visit to Bristol.

Lord Ryder glared at the girl. She was bedraggled and muddy, too tall, and if her face and neck were anything to go by, too thin. A strand of straight hair had escaped from her hood and was falling over one of her brown eyes, allowing rain to drip down her nose. He frowned and looked closer, a long white hand suddenly going up to jerk the concealing hood from her forehead. "I thought I knew you! I saw you at Magistrate Bulmore's house, did I not?"

Anabel was nonplussed. She imagined herself clever in watching him while concealing herself behind a pillar in the hall, but evidently Lord Ryder's eyes were exceptionally keen.

He gave a twisted smile. "Running away from Harcourt Manor? I cannot say I blame you. I feel the same way about Mr. Bulmore. A more puffed up, overbearing, conniving, tedious, pompous..."

Anabel detested her uncle, but perversely she

10

was not prepared to hear a stranger reviling him. "It pleased you, sir, to break bread with him and it ill becomes you to speak against him now."

Lord Ryder's brows went up. "It did not please me at all and you are an ill-mannered slut. How dare you address your betters in such a tone! I could have you whipped!"

"I do not doubt it, sir. Your—fame—has spread even to us country clodpoles."

What his lordship might have answered was lost as a combination of hunger, excitement and exertion took their toll and Anabel swayed. Her self-disgust at such weakness was paramount and she strove to retain her grasp on consciousness, dashing her hood from her head so that the cold February rain might sting her back to reality. But she was overcome by a wave of nausea so violent that she was forced to abandon her defiant stance and sink back on to the stone wall, her bundle falling to the ground, her head in her hands.

She expected Lord Ryder to enter his carriage and leave her, since the stories she had heard recounted of him had never included one of compassion. She was therefore surprised when she felt a touch on her arm and found him proffering a silver flask from which he removed the lid.

She shook her head and he gave an angry exclamation. "Drink, woman! It will restore you."

"What is it?"

"For pity's sake! Does it matter what it is if it will help you?"

She looked up, full into his lordship's eyes which she was startled to realize were a piercing blue.

11

Somehow she had thought he would have black eyes. Black to match his soul!

His mobile lips twisted in a mocking grin. "You are no doubt imagining that I keep a phial of drugged liquor ready to render helpless any young female I find unchaperoned."

One of the postilions converted a giggle into a cough as Lord Ryder turned for a moment to view him. Then he resumed his stare at Anabel whom he had succeeded in making feel ridiculous.

"I shall recover without the aid of your drink, my lord. Besides, I have not eaten since yesterday and on an empty stomach..."

"Good God! No food at all?"

"An apple only. I had no time..."

"What a typically stupid way to arrange an escape," snapped Lord Ryder.

"Typical of what?" asked Anabel in icy calm.

"Of an idiotic female," replied his lordship, in no way put out by her manner.

Anabel almost shook with indignation. "I was sent for by...by Mrs. Bulmore. The servant woke me very early. My...Mrs. Bulmore had a headache."

"Good!" exclaimed his lordship in tones of extreme satisfaction. "I hope it is something infectious and that the entire family will be forced to endure as much suffering as they inflicted on me during my, mercifully, short stay."

Anabel opened her mouth to administer another reproof, but Lord Ryder spoke first, his eyes narrowing as he looked down at her. "I do not wonder at your running away. What position did you hold in the family? Governess? Have the abominable Bulmores produced further offspring? Ladies' maid?"

Anabel closed her lips tightly and Lord Ryder shrugged. Then he swore softly as the rain increased, beating on his wide-brimmed beaver hat and soaking the velvet collar of his long greatcoat.

"Get up!" he said abruptly.

"I shall do no such thing. I am tired and I intend to remain seated until I feel like moving and..."

Anabel's speech ended in a gasp as his lordship grabbed her wrist, jerking her to her feet and propelling her toward his post chaise. She had never let go of her box and found it impossible to pull herself free. Both postilions were peering round, clearly enjoying the spectacle. All the stories she had heard about Lord Ryder tumbled about her brain, and at the door of the chaise she put one foot against the side and pushed back hard.

"Give me a hand, curse you!" grated Lord Ryder and a small man in black leaned from the coach, looked impassively into Anabel's face and pushed aside her foot with his and took her other arm.

Anabel's strength waned and with an exclamation of hopelessness she half fell into the chaise and sank onto its softly upholstered seat. Ryder yelled an instruction to the postilion, walked to the back of the coach with her bundle, then sprang in beside her and the coach rolled on its way.

"You will hear more of your behavior," said Anabel, fury thinning her voice into a spear of protest. "This is 1796, not the dark ages! Abduction is a crime!"

Lord Ryder coolly removed his hat and tossed it carelessly to the floor where it lay damply at their feet. "Move over, Cooper. There is ample room for three as thin as ourselves."

Cooper, who Anabel guessed was his lordship's valet, endeavored to squeeze himself into an even smaller space while Lord Ryder mopped at his collar with a piece of screwed-up newspaper.

He then looked at Anabel who turned to meet his gaze. She could not maintain her look for more than an instant. In spite of the calm tones of Lord Ryder's voice she was startled to see that his eyes contained even more rage than when she had almost overset his carriage.

He looked as if he hated her, and some of the more lurid tales she had read of dissolute and sadistic gentlemen came to plague her imagination. They would have to stop somewhere for horses and at the first opportunity she would escape. She held more tightly to her box. That must remain with her. It was her insurance against starvation. The small front wheels descended with a spine-jarring bump into a rut across the road where some farmer habitually led his cattle and Anabel's box dug into the Viscount's leather-breeched knee.

"What in hell have you got in there?" he demanded. "Don't tell me you've run off with some of the Bulmore treasure!"

With a swift movement he grabbed the box and pulled it from her grasp. She made frantic efforts to retrieve it and in the limited space her elbow jabbed Cooper's ribs, making him gasp.

The Viscount laughed without mirth. "Madam,

14

if you do not instantly be still I shall halt my coach and give you a lesson you will not easily forget."

His tone sent a frisson of fear over Anabel's body and abruptly she stopped her struggles. The Viscount's long, white fingers released the catch and he opened the box to stare in astonishment.

"Artist's materials. Is that all?"

Anabel did not answer and again the Viscount laughed. "You risked your life beneath my horses' hooves for this motley collection of worthless items! Are you mad?"

"I think it is you who are mad," retorted Anabel in low tones, "and excessively rude besides."

"How fascinating," said his lordship, as if she had not spoken. "It is a long time since I came across a situation which intrigued me more. In fact," he continued, "it is an enternity since I discovered anything which interested me at all."

"I have heard that *ennui* is a disease much favored by society loungers," said Anabel.

She felt Cooper's body stiffen. There was a brief silence during which the Viscount's anger was almost tangible.

"I have called men out for less," he remarked.

"I do not doubt it, sir."

"I may find it necessary to administer a reproof more suited to a woman. Do you doubt that, Madam Firebrand?"

"No insult you offered me would surprise me, sir, after the way you have treated me."

Anabel remained motionless as the Viscount turned again to stare at her. "What insult? I have insisted you ride in my carriage. You should be

15

grateful. I have probably saved you from lung fever. She should be grateful, should she not, Cooper?"

"Indeed, sir," agreed the valet.

"Naturally you would say anything he wanted," flashed Anabel. "You are paid to serve him and I must say I am sorry for you. I, however, am at liberty to speak honestly and you, my lord, are an arrogant fellow."

Again Cooper stiffened. Lord Ryder replied in a tone he might have used in dealing with someone of weak intellect. "Such high ropes do not sit well upon a woman whose very existence must depend on pleasing those who give her succor." He closed the box with a snap and replaced it on Anabel's knees. "You have not yet answered my question. In what capacity did you toil for the Bulmores? Ah! I have it! You taught drawing to their unwed daughter." He chuckled. "Did they think to catch a husband by adding to her tedious accomplishments?" His chuckle developed into a harsh laugh. "As if they stood a chance of riveting me to such a one. I, who have had the pick of the nation's most lovely and wealthy women since I was a youth."

Anabel gasped. "What overweening vanity!"

Cooper slumped, evidently deciding that the storm which the young woman was provoking was inevitable.

But Lord Ryder spoke in reasonable accents. "Is it vain to acknowledge the truth? I inherited as a child and have since had armies of women trying to trap me into wedlock. I did not choose. it thus. It happened."

"It is a situation you could have ended by marrying someone of birth and wealth since apparently you could select a bride from every family boasting a daughter," said Anabel.

"Marriage! It is not for me!" sneered the Viscount. "At first I was far too busy enjoying the advantages of unlimited means. Then I had ample opportunity to observe the shallow nature of womankind. I have seen men cuckolded, disillusioned, even destroyed. Quite strong males of my circle have been weakened by incessant demands from wives and offspring." The Viscount shuddered. "Thank you, madam, but I intend to live and die in single state."

"What a mercy that will be for the race of women," retorted Anabel.

"You really are a very saucy female," said Lord Ryder. "It is a great shame your looks do not match your spirit. You could have anticipated a most amusing and profitable time in London."

Anabel spoke quietly. "What makes you think that only a man can eschew marriage? I tell you, sir, that I would not enter into a match with any male. I have suffered too greatly..."

She stopped, wishing she had not said so much.

The Viscount sounded intrigued. "Pray proceed! What has happened to you? I wonder...there is a Bulmore son. Has he been making sport of you?"

He swiveled round and took her chin in strong fingers. In the cramped space she was forced to view him at such close quarters that she could see the soft hairs on his upper lip and the incipient lines spawned by his excesses. His eyes searched her face and for a long moment she returned his stare, before lowering her lids.

"Your eyes are lovely," exclaimed the Viscount. "Why did I not notice before? Brown eyes, flecked with gold! Look at me!"

Anabel tried to keep her lids down, but as if mesmerized she found herself once more gazing into Lord Ryder's blue eyes. After another long look he released her and she rubbed the soft skin where his fingers had gripped.

"I see innocence in you," pronounced his lordship. "Remarkable! How few females forced to earn their bread in the homes of the rich can have escaped molestation? It is perhaps fortunate that you are not endowed with beauty—always excepting your eyes, of course—but I daresay you keep them veiled in the presence of gentlemen."

Anabel was searching for a reply sufficiently scathing when there was a shout from one of the postilions and Lord Ryder said, "Good! They have sighted the stage. I shall stop it and you may continue your journey to London without my presence to annoy you."

Anabel turned then to look into the mocking face. All his talk, his threats, his questions had been simply a diversion. He had always meant to overtake the stage coach and be rid of her.

She gave an exaggerated sigh of relief. "Thank you, sir. I daresay we shall not meet again."

"Most unlikely," agreed his lordship, carelessly.

"I do not think we shall move in the same circles, Miss Drawing Mistress."

Anabel bit back a retort. In any case she would have found coherent speech impossible as she bounced between the two men as the postilions whipped up the horses and overtook the stage on a stretch of road Anabel considered dangerously narrow. They galloped on until the way became even more restricted when they pulled to a halt and waited for the stagecoach to stop.

The driver began to bellow a practiced stream of scurrilous comments regarding the postilions, the horses and the passengers of the postchaise. Anabel covered her ears, but Lord Ryder grinned in evil appreciation. "I thought I knew them all," he commented laconically. "Fascinating!"

In a leisured fashion he retrieved his hat, opened the chaise door and stepped into the road. He then untied Anabel's bundle from the back of the chaise and was in time to put out a saving hand as her foot became trapped in her heavy damp skirt.

"So good of you to take so much trouble, sir!"

"Not at all, madam! I would not forgo the amusement of seeing the play to the finish."

She stuffed her box under one arm and her bundle under the other and marched to the stage. The driver glared down at her and the guard added his own remarks upon the situation.

"I need to go to London," explained Anabel, "and I wish to travel inside. I am already quite wet."

There was a pause during which Anabel had time to note that the Viscount had not yet entered his coach, but was standing, one foot on the step, watching her.

Apparently the guard had simply been drawing enough breath to make it clear that not only was it impossible to travel inside, but also that there was no room on the top. Anabel glanced up at the hostile faces of the outside passengers who looked miserably soaked. She was appalled. "But, please, I must get to London. I . . . I cannot return home . . ."

"Ho! Is that so!" said the guard. "And why would that be, I wonder. What you done? You got something in that there box you shouldn't have?"

Anabel flinched at his hectoring manner which, like that of Lord Ryder, had probably been induced by her plain dark stuff gown and thick, serviceable cloak—both unfashionable and shabby.

She stifled her first answer and said, "I have done no wrong, sir. But I must go to London."

"Not on this coach, you don't, my girl. As soon as the chaise moves we drive on."

"Hold hard!" The cry came from Lord Ryder in a voice which coachman and guard instantly recognized as commanding. The coachman tightened his grip on the six pairs of reins and held his long whip high.

The Viscount sauntered to the guard. In his hand he held a golden guinea. "Will this assist you to find room for her?"

The guard licked his lips and looked regretfully at the gold. "Beggin' your pardon, sir, but I couldn't squeeze a kitten on. I've got all my passengers—every one."

The Viscount added a second guinea and the guard looked hopefully up at the outside passengers who stared back belligerently. "Sorry, sir, I got two more than I should have already."

Lord Ryder was not an easy man to deny. "If the lady is on your waybill it is your duty to make room for her."

"She ain't on it." The guard's astonishment was genuine. "I told you, sir, I got all my passengers—and more. She never booked a seat."

Lord Ryder turned inquiring brows to Anabel, who flushed. "I—did not know I should. I thought one stopped the coach and paid."

The guard shook his head at such ignorance and climbed back aboard. "Now, sir, if you'll move your po'chay we'll get on our way. We're running late as it is and my passengers are not pleased—not pleased at all. Especially as they had to walk up Tog Hill."

A rumble of angry agreement came from the outside passengers as Lord Ryder added a third guinea. The guard almost wept. "I tell you there's no room—unless..."

"Yes?" inquired the Viscount politely.

"She could travel in the rumble-tumble—and for half fare."

Anabel stared. "What is that?"

The guard touched his hat, climbed down, and led the way to the rear of the stage. "The rumble-tumble—the conveniency—the basket at the back. Course it's not very comfortable and there's a fair bit o' luggage in it, but 'tis better than walking."

Lord Ryder peered into the large basket. "Anyone who rides this must get badly shaken and knocked about."

The guard's eyes gleamed greedily as he stared at the Viscount's closed fist. "Well, most folks that use it are used to rough living, sir, and 'tis better than walking, like I said."

His lordship looked at Anabel who returned his gaze disdainfully. "If that is all that is offered then I accept," she said. "As for you, my lord, you can put your guineas away. If it is legal to ride in the basket and I can pay the fare there will be no need for bribery."

The guard began a spluttered protest and an outside passenger yelled, "Are we to wait all day in this confounded rain?"

Lord Ryder shrugged. "The lady will not be using the basket."

He forestalled any argument by tossing the guard a guinea.

The man grinned. "Thanks, sir. It's a pleasure to meet a real gentleman. Now, if you would be so obliging as to move your po'chay..."

Lord Ryder turned to Anabel. "Get back into my carriage."

"I will not. I demand to be accommodated on the stage!"

The driver intervened, bending from his lofty eminence to offer advice. "Now, miss, you'd be awful bruised. Milord is right. Do as he says."

"Sound reasoning," commented Lord Ryder. He lowered his voice. "Moreover, madam, if you do not obey me I shall pick you up in front of this entire company and carry you."

The sparkle of anticipation in the guard's eyes did more to persuade Anabel than anything said by Lord Ryder. She would travel on with him and escape later. She turned to him to express her loathing of his high-handed action and stopped as she surprised a glimmer in his eyes she could not fathom. If he had not the reputation of a merciless rake she might have mistaken it for respect.

She marched to the post chaise, head high, and climbed in beside Cooper who stared ahead impassively. Then the Viscount squeezed into his corner and the carriage was driven on.

Two

FOR A MILE OR TWO as the horses pulled the light coach through increasingly heavy rain no one spoke.

Anabel glanced from the window occasionally, making sure that she turned her eyes only to Cooper's side.

His lordship broke the silence. "Gratifying though it is to discover a woman who is able to hold her peace I think if we are to journey together we should at least exchange names."

"I know yours," said Anabel coldly. "You are Viscount Ryder, head of your family and exceedingly rich."

"Ah. I see there was talk in Bulmore's household. From your reply I may guess that my chief claim to notice is my large fortune. I daresay little, if indeed any, mention was made of my talents."

Anabel found it difficult to shrug in the confines of the carriage. "I heard some word of various skills at fisticuffs, swordsmanship, gun play and other unimportant diversions."

The Viscount laughed softly. "Such diversions have saved my life more than once."

"So I believe, sir. I am aware that you choose

a violent form of existence, but it is one which could not appeal to anyone of discerning taste."

"And you, madam, are of such taste?"

"I enjoy matters of the mind rather than the body."

The Viscount allowed her words to drop into a void which was more eloquent than speech and she was stung to continue, "I daresay you think I have little choice in my mode of living."

She had turned to look at him and Lord Ryder grinned unpleasantly. "I know nothing of the problems of the serving orders. Perhaps now you would favor me with your name."

Anabel breathed hard. "I am Miss Anabel Ha-Hyde!"

"How do you do, Miss Anabel Ha-Hyde. What an unusual name."

"I did but cough, sir. I am called Hyde."

"I trust you have not taken a chill. Truly, Miss Hyde, if you are of so delicate a disposition it would not have suited you to ride in the basket—or even on top of the stage."

Anabel was almost overset by the sudden memory of his lordship's eyes as he had insisted on her accompanying him.

She searched for a belated expression of gratitude, but he spoke first. "Tell me, Cooper, have you packed anything which would allay Miss Hyde's distressing cough?"

"No, sir, I fear not. But I daresay some inn woman can find a linctus."

"I require no medicine!" snapped Anabel.

"Your cough is so quickly conquered?" asked Lord Ryder in oversolicitous tones.

Anabel had an impulse to claw at the white hand which lay on Lord Ryder's knee. She stared at the well-tended nails, the smooth whiteness of the skin and her lip curled before she recalled the strength in his fingers.

The coach jolted and lurched as the wheels slid on the muddy road and the Viscount cursed gently. "Never again will I believe a country squire who tells me of a superlative stud horse for sale. I should be in town preparing for an evening of amusement—a little music, perhaps—maybe a dance—or conversation of the sort which is so diverting to such as myself—idle butterflies of the social round, Miss Hyde. I fear that none of it would appeal to a bluestocking like you."

"You, sir, are not so featherbrained as you pretend; and if I were a bluestocking I might hold your interest as I know that my—that Miss Bulmore did not."

"So you heard of our conversation. How fascinating. And you thought me intelligent. I call that handsome of you!"

Anabel was saved from answering by Cooper who burst forth, "His lordship is a collector of fine art. He has many articles of great antiquity and lots of pictures..."

"Most of which were probably amassed by his ancestors," sneered Anabel.

"Oh, no!" protested the Viscount. "I have purchased a great deal. I have paintings by Sir Thomas Lawrence and Monsieur Fragonard..."

"Sir Thomas I respect," declared Anabel, "but I know the other man to be a painter of quite licentious performance."

The valet gasped and Lord Ryder said, "I purchase what is beautiful and famous, but I also encourage the new artists. I have work by the young Mr. Turner..."

"I hear no woman's name among your eulogies," said Anabel frostily.

"Women! Painting!" The valet was startled again into speech. "It's not a respectable world for a female!"

"Well, *I* intend to enter it. I have long admired Louise Vigée-Lebrun. She is an artist of merit and a perfectly reputable character."

"I never heard of her," muttered Cooper.

"An excellent artist specializing in portraits of women and children," expounded the Viscount.

Anabel spoke eagerly. "You know of her—perhaps you have met her."

"I have not had the pleasure, but I have seen her work. It is good."

"I hope I may do as well," cried Anabel.

His lordship's eyes strayed to Anabel's box. "So that is why you were so fearful for the safety of your materials. Am I to understand that you intend to set yourself up in London as a portrait painter?"

"Yes, sir."

"You must be wanting in wit," said Lord Ryder with cruel frankness. "Madame Vigée-Lebrun is the daughter of an artist and married to a dealer. Pray, who will sponsor you?"

"I need no sponsor! I am capable of finding a lodging and advertising my profession."

"Good God! Where do you propose to place these advertisements? What terminology will you use? And what kind of applicants will you meet?" His mouth twisted in a significant grin.

Anabel felt the color rise to her face. "Not all the world is wicked!"

"I made no such insinuation, madam, and if you interpret my astonishment in so accurate a fashion it can only be because you know and share my doubts about your intentions."

Anabel was reduced to a seething silence. She had not been out in the world, but her isolation at her uncle's unwelcoming home had led her to indulge in much reading. She had learned enough from newspapers and magazines to know that London was no place for a woman to wander alone.

"Well, madam?"

The Viscount was insisting on a reply and she said in low tones, "I think you make sport of me, but you will see. I shall prove to you..."

"Spare me! You will prove nothing to me for it is unlikely in the extreme that we shall inhabit the same society, even on the fringes. When we arrive in London I shall be thankful to set you down and you may go wherever you please. It is nothing to me."

Anabel was disappointed beyond reason. She felt anger well in her. "You asked questions which I answered and now you treat me with disdain."

"Disdain?" The Viscount sounded contemplative. "Rather resignation. It is obvious that you are an obstinate woman who will not be swayed by advice which I offer—in your best interests, I assure you—and therefore I see nothing to be gained by discussing your plans."

Anabel lapsed into silence which was broken only when they stopped at one of the staging inns and ate luncheon. The postilions removed their sodden garments and Anabel saw for the first time the blue and gold livery of the Ryder family.

The men touched their forelocks to their master before seeking food in the warmth of the kitchen. Anabel removed her heavy cloak and straightened her cramped back. "I wonder you keep the same postilions throughout the journey, Lord Ryder. Surely they deserve a rest."

The Viscount allowed Cooper to relieve him of his coat and hat and handed Anabel's cloak to him before replying. "I choose those who serve me with care and I pay them well. The riders are men of exceptional stamina who possess the skill to nurture my highly bred cattle."

As Cooper left the private room bespoken by his lordship he threw Anabel a glance which was eloquently beseeching, but she chose to ignore his mute appeal for discretion. "Ah, your horses! They are more important than human beings!"

The Viscount strolled to the fireplace and kicked a coal into flame. "My postilions feel a love for my horses equal to my own. If they did not I should not employ them."

Anabel continued in her determination to provoke him. "That I do not doubt, sir."

"You have an inordinate interest in the condition of my servants which causes me to wonder again about your position in Harcourt Manor. You did not answer my question!"

Anabel became busy trying to straighten the folds of her gown which had grown sadly creased. "Is it possible for me to wash somewhere?" she asked.

"I am sure it is. What position did you hold?"

Anabel stared down at the toes of her half boots, trying to cope with the flood of sensation and memory which his words conjured. She thought of the years in which she had lived on the edges of the Bulmore family, scarcely ever sharing their pastimes, driven always deeper into her inner resources for the sustenance of a spirit they had failed to break. What position had she held?

"I was a kind of companion to Miss Bulmore," she said at last.

"And you have enough humanity left to think of postilions. Amazing! It proves what I have long held to be true—that females are capable of ridiculous extremes of self-abasement."

Anabel looked up quickly, her nostrils flaring. "There is a vast difference between such humiliation and a will to survive. The wise tree bends with the wind. If I had not been compliant I would have been broken."

For an instant the Viscount looked startled, then he laughed softly. "You have succeeded in surprising me again, Miss Hyde. *Incroyable!* But why did you not seek another position?"

Anabel shrugged as she dissembled. "One household is much the same as any other to such women as myself."

31

"You are an astonishing blend of wisdom and ignorance, madam!"

"What mean you, sir?"

"You have instincts of survival which would benefit a warrior, yet you did not question the propriety of entering a private chamber with a man who is a stranger to you."

Anabel frowned. "You have been at pains to inform me that my dubious charms would not tempt you to molest me, my lord." She swept him a deep curtsey. "I do promise you that had I found favor in your lordship's sight I would have behaved in a vastly different manner."

Anger flickered in his eyes and Anabel felt a savage satisfaction. Then the Viscount's face became bland as he handed her a card. "Pray read the bill of fare so that we may eat. I do not wish to waste time."

Anabel was shown to a small room where she was able to sponge some of the travel stains from her person and garments and comb her hair, after which they lunched off boiled fowl with egg sauce and spiced apple pudding which Anabel devoured hungrily. She had eaten cheesecakes and drunk milk at one of the post houses, but it had made little impression on the void in her stomach.

The Viscount ate with discretion and she compared him favorably with her uncle and his cronies who appeared to encompass a wish to grow as obese in body as they were dull in wit. But Lord Ryder drank deeply of the claret brought by the host after a waiter had been despatched back to the cellar with an inferior blend which had drawn forth some imaginative criticisms from his lordship.

Anabel took only one glass, preferring freshly made barley water, and Lord Ryder's brows lifted. "Afraid of getting intoxicated and helpless in my power?"

"I have found it discreet to keep my mind clear at all times," rejoined Anabel in a voice which sounded prim even to herself.

The Viscount stared at her over the rim of his glass before placing it on the table with infinite care. "Have you had experiences which would promote such a lackluster attitude?"

A flush mantled her cheeks as she thought of her cousin Miles's clumsy efforts to make love to her and Lord Ryder's brows drew together above his eyes. "I assure you, Miss Hyde, that I have not yet been found sufficiently wanting in manhood to render it necessary to seduce females in a state of intoxication."

"I well believe you, sir. I daresay one as well versed as yourself in worldly ways and, we must not forget, as heavily endowed as yourself with worldly goods, will always find some idiot female ready to hurl her willing body into your arms."

"By God, madam, you act as if you were a duchess! I trust you will modify your behavior to your clients. Always supposing you obtain some!"

He rose and moments later Anabel was back in the post chaise, again seated between his lordship and Cooper, and the sound of hooves, the turn of the wheels on the wet road and the incessant beating of the rain took on so dreamlike a quality that she began to wonder if she had imagined the halt at the inn.

They were through the town of Reading and London only thirty-five miles ahead when the chaise was pulled to an unexpected stop. There were sounds of slithering hooves, declaiming voices and a scraping of wood upon wood which was followed by shouts of rage. Cooper climbed down into the road and returned a moment later. "The river has risen and the bridge is awash to a depth of several feet. There are also logs and boulders brought down by the floodwater and blocking the way."

The Viscount sighed. "Surely it is not beyond the power of some local farmer to bring work-horses to clear the obstacles."

"Even if they did, sir, we still couldn't get through. Several other carriages are ahead and they are all trying to turn back. One was almost swept away."

Lord Ryder joined his valet in the driving rain and returned looking dark with fury as he climbed into the chaise and threw himself beside Anabel. Cooper followed him.

"I regret to inform you, madam," grated the Viscount, "that we must return to Reading to bespeak beds for the night. Damn the weather and God damn all Bulmores. I only pray that the storm will have abated enough for us to reach London tomorrow."

"Since you appear to be on such familiar terms with God I daresay He will oblige you."

Lord Ryder breathed heavily. "I do not think I

have ever before met a female whose departure will give me more pleasure."

Anabel held her tongue, but her eyes sparkled with rebellion at a fate which had led her to being closeted with a man who seemed to possess all the faults she most abominated. The fact that she was indebted to him made her more resentful, an emotion which she could see was shared by his lordship toward herself. When he reentered the chaise their eyes had met briefly and she had almost flinched at the look he had thrown her.

He hates discipline, however indirectly imposed; he is childish, she assured herself.

However, there was nothing childish in the way his lordship overrode all objection by the host of the Bear Inn at Reading. The corpulent landlord wrung his hands imploringly. "I haven't got an inch to put you, sir. The weather's so bad lots of travelers have stopped unexpected. Please, sir, it's not a bit of use going on at me!"

Lord Ryder's reply to such ill-conceived protest was to throw a handful of coins on to the taproom table and wait. The landlady bustled forward and scooped them expertly into her apron pocket.

"Just you and your good lady make yourselves comfy in my parlor and we'll find a room for you in no time." She turned to her husband. "Get that pair out of the bedchamber at the back. They can have our room. Oh, shut your noise, man, we can sleep in the kitchen—if we get any sleep at all," she ended, as the outer door opened and a wave of clamoring travelers surged in demanding succor.

Anabel tried to make her voice heard as she

35

declared that she could not share a room with Lord Ryder and was relieved to see him follow the landlady and point out that he and his "sister" must have two bedchambers.

The look of anguish flung back at his wife by the landlord brought an hysterical giggle to Anabel's lips and Cooper, who stood waiting with his master's valise and Anabel's bundle, gave her a concerned glance.

She put out a hand. "Give me my clothes, please."

The landlady paused and took full note of Anabel for the first time, and her opinion of her serviceable garments, knotted bundle and battered box was clear in her expression. "Did I hear milord call you his sister, ma'am?" she asked with pointed courtesy, ignoring for the moment the vociferous demands of a lady with two pug dogs.

"That is so." Lord Ryder stepped to Anabel's side. "My foolish sister thought to elope with a young man of no consequence and borrowed a kitchen maid's garb. I am taking her home."

Anabel opened her mouth to protest, then shut it again as she recognized her ambiguous position. Lord Ryder smiled equably at her, twin devils dancing in his eyes. "You really are a naughty girl," he chided. "Papa will punish you as you deserve when we arrive home."

"What a dreadful thing to do," said the landlady. She bent her ear to Lord Ryder's whisper and money changed hands as she handed him something.

Anabel waited only until they were seated in

a corner of the parlor awaiting supper before she burst out, "Eloping indeed! How dare you malign me! As if I would do anything so bird-witted!"

The Viscount's humor subsided as the room was invaded by the lady with the pug dogs and several other travelers of consequence who could not be accommodated in the eating room and were too well bred for the kitchen.

"It is not my fault we are stranded here," hissed Anabel into his scowling visage.

"Did I say it was?"

"No, but you have a way of glaring at me as if I had manufactured the situation."

"Do not be absurd. The weather is not your fault, but your presence complicates matters. As it turns out, you are to have the largest bedchamber while I..."

Anabel found exquisite satisfaction in asking sweetly, "Are you not housed to suit your grandeur, sir?"

He looked at her through lowered lashes. "I could find it in me to punish you for your impudence."

She leaned forward. "Are you, as it were, 'hoist by your own petard,' my lord? Having claimed me for a sister had you to allow me the best room?"

His lordship's hand went up, then he clenched his fist and Anabel sat back, startled by the fury in his bearing.

"I was jesting," she said weakly.

"I also like a jest, madam! I begin to regret calling you sister. What would you have done had I had us placed in the same room?"

"There is no question of it!"

"No? You saw how quickly I conquered with money. Much may be accomplished by such methods."

He stared at her in such grim anger that she was shaken and spoke placatingly. "You have had a most wearing time lately. I am sorry I added to your annoyance. If you are cross it is understandable..."

"Pray, do not trouble yourself to understand me, madam!"

They fell silent as the waiter put plates before them. Lord Ryder poked about in his with an exploratory fork. "Stewed rabbit as I live and breathe."

Anabel did not venture a reply, but applied herself to her stew, while his lordship demanded, and received, a raised ham pie and almond cheesecakes. He almost forgave the inn its fare when the landlord brought him a bottle of good port kept only, he explained, for visiting nobility.

Anabel drank coffee and sighed with repletion. "I had hoped to be in London tonight, but I am thankful in the circumstances to be so comfortable."

"Will not someone be waiting for your arrival?"

"No, indeed. I am going to fend for myself."

"Where will you be staying?"

A wary look spread over Anabel's face and the Viscount snorted with impatience. "God, what a suspicious woman you are! I am but making polite conversation."

"I see." Anabel poured more coffee and offered

a cup to Lord Ryder who shook his head and reached for the port.

Anabel was able to observe him at leisure and saw that if his face were not set in such hard lines he would be accounted handsome. His unpowdered brown hair sprang in natural waves from a well-shaped head and was loosely contained behind by a narrow black ribbon. She had thought him thin, but realized that his height created the illusion. His perfectly tailored coat of midnight-blue broadcloth was moulded to muscular shoulders and his legs, stretched out to one side of the table, were long and lithe.

When she looked up she found him watchful, blue eyes diamond sharp. "Well, madam, do I pass muster?"

She blushed. "I did not mean to stare. We have sat together for hours and I had not seen you properly."

"Oh? What about in Master Bulmore's house? You were peering at me from behind a pillar in the hall."

"It was dim . . . Mr. Bulmore economizes on candles . . . I was curious to see what . . . what manner of man . . ."

"Pray continue, Miss Hyde."

She remained silent, gnawing at her lower lip, and he supplied, "You were curious to see what man Mr. Bulmore had lured to his house with false promises of a bloodstock stallion so that he might promote his odious daughter's charms."

"I would not have put it so."

"I daresay not. Women have a flair for dissembling. And talking of women, I have not yet mentioned the senior Bulmore female. How you could bear to spend an hour beneath the roof of such a creature as she...!"

Again Anabel felt she should defend her kin. Her aunt was, after all, the sister of her late papa, yet she could not find a word in her favor and said weakly, "I had no choice in where I spent my days."

"Nonsense!" Anabel felt her anger rising at the Viscount's contempt. "You could have left. You have run away now—why not earlier? And why escape in such a fashion anyway? How old are you?"

He snapped the questions at her so shatteringly fast that she stammered, "T...twenty, sir. Almost one and twenty."

"How many years have you borne with that family?"

"Mind your own business," cried Anabel, so loudly that several occupants of the parlor turned round in surprise.

"It is of no concern of yours, sir," she hissed. "Tomorrow, pray heaven, we shall part and never meet again."

"With your prayers added to mine I am sure the river will go down in the night."

She pressed her lips together and shot him a look of resentment.

He smiled triumphantly. "It is quite a joy to anger you, my dear. You look positively fetching when enraged."

Again he poured himself some wine. "So you are to fend for yourself in London. What plans have you made?"

"Quite enough, thank you!" She was more abrupt than she meant because she had no idea of where she would stay, though she would have died rather than admit it to the Viscount. How could she have made proper arrangements when all letters were carried first to her aunt and uncle who opened every one? To collect funds for her escape had taken all her ingenuity. Her pin money was niggardly and she had needed to spend hours darning and mending to save the expense of new stockings and gloves.

This brought a sudden thought and she asked in determinedly casual tones, "Have you any idea of the cost of staying here?"

"Oh, very little," he answered carelessly.

"But how much would you think?"

"Short of capital, Miss Hyde? I will pay our shot."

"That you will not, sir! I will not be beholden to you. At least, not more than I am already. As it is I have saved the stage fare. Unless..."

He looked at her with a dangerous gleam. "Of course, you are not about to insult me by tendering me the fare."

"N...no, sir," she stammered, thankful to have bitten off the offer before it was expressed.

"As for the cost of staying here," said the Viscount casually, "that will depend on how soon the bridge is cleared and we may proceed. You must have some idea from your previous journeyings."

Anabel's puzzlement did not escape him. "When you went to work for the Bulmores," prompted the

Viscount with deceptive gentleness. "I take it you did not walk there."

Again Anabel was thrown into memory. Herself in 1784, a weeping eight-year-old, journeying in the care of a nursemaid who had small affection for the thin, plain child she was to deliver on her way to a new position, the Bulmores having decided that she could share their own nursery staff. She remembered her beautiful mother, her frequent laughter, her joy in dancing, her uncritical love for her changeling child. Mama had grown silent and morose in the weeks before she died. Anabel knew now that this was because of the baby she carried and the illness it brought. Neither her mother nor her infant brother had survived the birth more than a few hours, and weeks later her distraught father had broken his neck riding recklessly in the hunting field.

How could a man with so charming a disposition as her father have sprung from the same womb as had borne her Aunt Bulmore? She was sour, mean and falsely welcoming to the small girl.

Anabel had no notion that her painful musings had brought a haunting look of regret to her gold-flecked eyes and she was surprised when the Viscount said softly, "How long were you with them?"

"Them? I beg your pardon, sir? What was your question?"

"I asked how long you were with the abominable Bulmores?"

"Too long," said Anabel and closed her lips firmly.

Lord Ryder shrugged. "Well, your shot here,

42

with vails, won't amount to much above half a guinea if we can move on tomorrow."

"A half guinea!" Anabel was appalled. The five guineas she had amassed would not last long at this rate. A prickle of fear caught her. The sooner she obtained lodging and work the better. Suddenly she felt desperately weary and Lord Ryder, who seemed to have an uncanny ability for sensing her moods said, "Bed, I think, Miss Hyde."

He called for lights and together they were conducted to the upper floor where the maidservant opened the door of a spacious room and bade her good night.

Anabel entered and was surprised to find the Viscount close behind her. She said distantly, "I should prefer it if you left at once, my lord."

"You still have not answered my question regarding your lodging in London."

"What is it to you?"

"Let us say that I am curious. It is increasingly obvious that you are not the usual type of upper servant. Companion to Miss Bulmore, you called yourself. Why did I discover you sitting forlornly upon a wall, carrying a bundle like a traveling tinker?"

Anabel took a deep breath. "Sir, I am grateful—truly grateful—for the help you have rendered me. I do not know how I should have gone on without you, but that does not give you the right to...pry into my affairs."

Lord Ryder's jaw moved as he clenched his teeth; then he said softly, "No one has ever before accused me of prying, Miss Hyde. It is the second time I have wished you were a man."

"Well, I am a woman, but not helpless. I shall look after myself, thank you."

"Have you ever been to London?"

"Once I passed through the outskirts."

"And do you imagine that gives you sufficient knowledge of the town to settle there alone?"

Anabel's temper rose. "Sir, I am an adult female. I am not . . . not a beauty . . ."—even in the midst of her fury it was hard to admit this truth—"and therefore am unlikely to meet any of the parasites who prey upon unprotected women..."

"Oh, you know about those, do you?" Lord Ryder's voice held mocking humor and Anabel grew angrier.

"I have read a lot, my lord."

He startled her by throwing back his head and giving a shout of mirth; then he stared into her eyes, his lips drawn back from a wolfish grin. "Do you really suppose a woman needs outstanding looks to be taken up by the harridans of London? You are a child in such matters. I did but ask your direction that I might offer advice. Do you think I have designs upon your virtue?"

Anabel's fingers itched to strike the amusement from his face. "No, sir, I think nothing of the kind. In any case, should anyone molest me I shall have no hesitation in defending myself in any means in my power."

"Indeed!" Lord Ryder looked speculatively at her; then with an abrupt movement he kicked the door shut.

"My lord..." cried Anabel as the Viscount advanced. The look in his eyes induced an alarming weakness about her knees and she stepped back. Then she straightened her shoulders and glared at him. "Open the door and leave instantly."

"Not until I have proved something," he said, as he moved with catlike grace and speed and slid an arm about her.

Three

FOR A MOMENT ANABEL remained rigid with anger, then she lifted her clenched hand and struck at the Viscount with all her strength. He was not quite quick enough to deflect the entire force of her blow and her knuckles caught his lip, drawing a fleck of blood.

Then she was imprisoned in the embrace of his right arm and he raised her face to his, his long fingers gripping her chin. Anabel stared into the blue eyes so near her own and for the first time in her life felt true fear. The events of the day scurried around her brain and she was brought to a full understanding of her situation.

She had allowed herself to be taken into the coach of a notorious rakehell, had traveled with him for a number of miles, had dined with him in a public inn, had not denied his assertion that she was his sister, and had sat by while he hired a bedchamber for her.

She was at his mercy and not a soul in the world would ever be convinced that she had not connived at what she was sure would be an assault upon her honor.

"Let me go!" she gasped.

She searched in vain for a sign of mercy in the Viscount's face. She felt he knew exactly what had passed through her mind and clearly it amused him. His lips were slightly parted in a grim smile and the cut she had inflicted was gleaming and red.

"Let you go? Why should I?"

"I shall scream for help!"

"Then I had best stop your mouth—like this!"

His lips came down on hers in a kiss which was searching and demanding and from her first wild resistance she felt a treacherous melting of her senses. Her experience of Miles's fumblings had not prepared her for the way the mouth of a man could move upon her own, drawing a response which existed outside her will. Her own lips parted and her breathing quickened. She sensed a sudden difference in Lord Ryder's gripping strength. He had begun the embrace with cruel amusement. Now it altered to a desire which owed nothing to a wish to punish her. The arm which had been like an iron band about her became an urgent caress. His hand left her chin and moved gently over her neck and spine.

Anabel's senses became a turmoil of outrage and newly discovered, scarcely understood, emotions which this stranger was dragging from deep within her. With a moan she began to struggle. For an instant he held her in a harder grip, then with an abruptness more shocking than a blow he thrust her back and stood a pace away, his eyes no longer mocking.

"My God, woman! I could swear you are an innocent, yet...!"

"Go," she begged. "Get out—leave me alone, my lord. I don't know what you believe me to be, but I...I..."

His voice was low. "I have never had any intent to besmirch your honor, madam. You angered me."

"I struck you out of fear!"

"I was not referring to the blow." He dismissed the suggestion contemptuously, and her cheeks burned. "I had it in mind to show you how disastrously easy it would be for me to take what I would from you. I was proving that your intention to settle in London in the manner you describe will bring you to ruin."

Lord Ryder seemed calmer now and his mouth twisted in a sardonic smile. "I intend to leave you unsullied, madam, I do assure you, but had I been another kind of man you might have had a sorry tale to tell."

Her tones were as low as his. "Had you been another kind of man, sir, I am sure I would not have accompanied you beyond the first posthouse this morning, for in spite of your reputation I believed I could trust you."

Lord Ryder's brows rose, then he laughed in genuine amusement. "Pray, Miss Hyde, do me the favor of keeping such an opinion to yourself when you reach London or I shall be a laughing stock. My standing will be quite spoiled if my enemies get to learn of my forbearance to you."

Anabel was shaking with fury and shame as she recalled how quickly she had responded to the

49

Viscount's kiss. He must suppose her wanton, yet still he professed to believe her innocent. He was beyond her comprehension.

She drew a long breath. "Leave me!" she commanded.

He bowed. "We shall meet in the morning."

There was an air of subtle derision about him which made her ache to rend him with words or blows, but she held her peace. Tomorrow she would rise at dawn and escape him. They would not meet again and she would forget that his presence gave her a curious sense of need.

Without another word Lord Ryder opened the chamber door, bowed once more, and snapped the door shut behind him. There was a slight click and Anabel leapt forward and tried the handle. She was locked in and she realized that the innkeeper's wife must have given him the key.

"Open this door, damn you!" she cried.

"Such language, Miss Hyde!" His ironical voice reached her from near the door. "I have no intention of allowing you to run from me. I said I would convey you to London and that is what I shall do. Sleep well!"

The sound of his retreating footsteps filled her with hate. Her fingers writhed in impotent rage. She ran to the window, but the small casement revealed a drop of some twenty feet. She slammed the window shut and with a feeling of inevitability looked around the room.

It was clean and comfortable and a linen press held her small supply of undergarments, while in a corner cupboard her other gown hung cleaned and pressed. She wondered how much Ryder had needed to pay to have this service performed on so busy a night.

It was odd to think that she found a greater degree of attention at a common inn than she had received in her own home. Until lately, she mused. Her aunt had suddenly begun to treat her with a little more care. Cold aggression had been muted, dislike cleverly suppressed. There had even been one or two treats, a few bits of lace to decorate her gowns.

Anabel's smile could not have been bettered by the Viscount. Her family had thought to bribe her into wedlock with Miles. They had allowed her to taste in small doses the life they promised with their lips if she married her cousin, while their cold eyes had told her conclusively that once she stepped into their trap she would be relegated once more to the background of their selfish lives.

She would get to London and since Lord Ryder insisted on taking her she would use him. Once there she was sure she could find a place to hide until her twenty-first birthday was past. Four months only she needed to complete her purpose and four months would she get in any way she must.

She began to peel off her clothes, removing her dark stuff dress and following it with the several petticoats which hung from her waist, giving her skirt some of the fullness which was fashionable lately without the aid of panniers. She thought of her cousin Drusilla's numerous petticoats of taffeta and silk and stared at her own plain cotton

51

with a certain satisfaction that she had sewn the gifts of lace to her undergarments where she only would see it. A small triumph, and childish, but anything which enabled her to score over her relatives was not to be despised.

Then her smile faded as she stared at herself in the damp-spotted cheval glass. She was so thin that she needed no corset to pull her into shape. She examined with inflexible frankness the angularity of her bone structure, her pale complexion and straight hair and wondered what had brought Lord Ryder to the point of desiring her. She turned sharply from her reflection, filled with disgust at them both.

She washed in water grown cold; another pinprick of annoyance laid at the Viscount's door, but the fire in the iron grate burned with soothing warmth and she snuggled into a downy mattress where the tumult of her brain conceded defeat and she slept.

Morning dawned with a slight easing of the rain, but the bridge was still impassable and Anabel faced the thought that she might have to spend another night at the inn.

The Viscount unlocked her door early and greeted her as calmly as if the scene in her bedchamber had never occurred. They descended to a mercifully empty parlor where they ate ham and boiled eggs in silence.

As Lord Ryder spread apricot preserve thickly upon toast he inquired in deeply solicitous tones, "Did you sleep well, Miss Hyde?"

Immediately suspicious of his motives she

glanced into his face which held a tinge of mockery—and something else; a flicker of real interest which suspended her scathing reply. "Yes, thank you, my lord. And you?"

"I also, thank you, in spite of a cupboard-sized room and a lumpy mattress."

"Oh!" His voice had been dispassionate, but she felt she owed him something for his sacrifice of the only good bed. "I was pleased to have my door secured. During the night I realized that drunken revelers attempted an entry."

Lord Ryder grinned malevolently. "Two incipient assaults in one night! Your charms have attracted much attention."

Anabel flushed angrily. "You are pleased to scorn me, sir! And I was only trying to be polite. You need not have locked me in. I am quite capable of looking after myself. I have been used to..."

"Used to what, Miss Hyde? Have you had to fend off the attacks of eager young bucks determined upon a new conquest?"

"No, sir, I have not!"

"Then what...? Ah, I have it. Young Bulmore— what is his name?"

"Miles Bulmore, sir."

She was curt, realizing that she had tacitly admitted his assumption to be correct. She recalled the time when Miles had taken her by surprise in the garden house and had planted his fleshy lips on hers, while his hands stroked clumsily at her bodice. She called for help and a gardener's boy had run in enabling her to escape. The boy was dismissed and Anabel was left to contemplate the fact that she had discovered her aunt well within hearing. That had been two weeks ago and confirmed her suspicion that anything Miles did would be condoned and encouraged by his parents, not excepting a forced seduction.

She shivered and saw that the Viscount watched her with a piercing interest. "Your thoughts bring you pain, Miss Hyde?"

She shrugged her thin shoulders. "It is happily behind me now. In London I shall be safe from the life I have led."

"Safe is not a word I would use in connection with your proposals for your future. I assume it would be useless for me to persuade you that you should return to Harcourt Manor."

She set her lips and it was his turn to shrug. He rose and strolled to the window. "Thank God the rain has stopped. Let us hope the bridge will soon be cleared. Tonight I should attend a rout at Her Grace of Stowebridge's residence in Grosvenor Square. She is ingenious at finding new ways to amuse her guests."

"I hope it remains fine for you! It would be dreadful if you should be bored by another night away from your pleasurable pursuits."

The Viscount turned and leaned negligently against the wall. "I can only suppose that your existence with the Bulmores to have been dull beyond belief if you find this inn even remotely distracting."

"I am thankful to say that I am never dull—or bored. So long as I have books and my painting I can find ample consolation in my own company."

Lord Ryder permitted himself a small yawn which he covered with his white hand. Anabel stared at the Mechlin lace ruffles on his shirt sleeves, the impeccable dark blue coat over a striped waistcoat and the discreetly slender gold watch chain and became unjustly angry that his appearance was attractive.

"I am thankful to say, sir, that I have not reached your depths of surfeit. How can you endure to live in so aimless and tedious a fashion?"

His lordship gave the question consideration, his brow furrowed slightly. "I wish I could answer you, but truly I cannot. I must conclude that I see no other life open to a gentleman of taste."

"That is nonsense! You appeared to be well endowed with wit"—here the Viscount favored her with a small bow—"and could occupy yourself with many rewarding subjects."

"Such as?"

"Well, there is science, for one. I have read of a man who is trying to discover a safer way to inoculate against the smallpox."

"Mr. Jenner appears to be managing well enough without my inexpert assistance and apart from offering myself as a subject for experimentation" —the Viscount wrinkled his brow—"but I fear I would be of no use. I was protected from the disease by the old method."

Anabel flushed. "You are absurd. I meant only that you should pursue some interesting study."

"And how do you know I do not?"

She was silent and Lord Ryder laughed softly. "Well, you are right, madam. I am an idle fellow."

"You should be ashamed. With all your advantages..."

"Good God! You begin to remind me of my Oxford tutors—and singularly tedious I found most of them."

The conversation was terminated by the entrance of several folk who grumbled loudly at being refused breakfast in their rooms and their clamor was increased when they realized that they were still prisoners at an inn they described as inadequate. Anabel decided that they were all as trivial as the Viscount and rose to return to her bedchamber.

At the parlor door she met one of Ryder's postilions who took letters from his master. To London hostesses, supposed Anabel. For such a purpose he was prepared to order his servant to find a way over the river on horseback and she glanced back at the Viscount with a curling lip.

He received her look with a sardonic grin, gave her a graceful bow, and reseated himself, calling for coffee.

The hours passed with excruciating slowness, made more unendurable for Anabel by the fear that her relatives were gaining time to pursue her. They must also be stranded somewhere on the dreadful road, but by two o'clock she was so nervous she resolved to abandon her intention to use the Viscount's chaise and set out to walk ways unfrequented by vehicles.

She and Lord Ryder were seated by the parlor window trying to ignore the lamentations of the other stranded travelers. In fact his lordship appeared to possess a supreme aptitude for behaving as if he were alone. He had read all available newspapers and magazines and lay back, legs stretched out, eyes closed.

Assuming that he slept Anabel began to rise. Instantly the Viscount's eyes opened and he regarded her between narrowed lids, a faint smile curving his mobile mouth.

"Going somewhere, my dear sister?"

She glared at him, then turned on a forced smile. "I thought I would take a turn about the inn."

Ryder's body tautened as he stretched. "I will accompany you."

"I would prefer to be alone!"

He looked at his gold watch, then through the window. "I should think we might be moving again shortly. Yes, I definitely will walk with you."

She was convinced he had guessed her intention. Probably he had been watching her covertly all day. It seemed to have become of vital importance to him that he should convey her to London. He evidently could not bear to be thwarted.

To her infinite relief it was announced ten minutes later that the road was clear and soon they were driving from the inn yard, the missing postilion having been replaced by a boy from the inn.

As they clattered over the cobbles a carriage driven at a reckless speed turned in and Anabel saw with a heart-stopping shock that it contained her cousin Miles. He looked in a vicious mood as he peered at the Viscount's coach. Had his eyes not been riveted on the crested door he must surely have looked up and seen her.

She drew back sharply and looked straight into Ryder's eyes. He spoke in casual fashion. "My dear Miss Hyde, you look alarmed. Do you know the man in the coach which passed?"

Anabel could not be certain that the Viscount had not seen and recognized Miles. She took refuge in a shrug. "Why should you think that?"

"Why indeed," he countered. "Yet you looked positively frightened. Who would go to such lengths for a serving woman, unless...! Oh, my dear Miss Hyde, what can you have done?"

Anabel's temper snapped. "I am not your dear Miss Hyde. I am not your *dear* anything—and I have done nothing wrong."

She breathed deeply, refusing to give her tormentor the further satisfaction of riling her. A company of farm laborers worked about the bridge. The waters had receded, leaving stones and mud which they were moving, and the Viscount rolled open his window and threw out a handful of silver coins. He chuckled as the men threw aside shovels and brooms to dive for them.

Anabel said, "You degrade them by throwing money at them."

"Do I? I would never have believed it. Why did they lose their dignity by scrabbling about like rats in a sewer?"

"They are probably hungry—their wives and children may need food."

Ryder looked amazed. "Is that so? They looked burly fellows to me. Perhaps I should have thrown gold. Pray, Miss Hyde, should we turn and offer them more money?"

Anabel seethed with fury. "You are intent upon making me seem foolish."

A wind sprang up and the muddy roads began to dry, forming ridges over which the coaches bumped and jolted. By the time they reached Hounslow Heath the clouds were darkening the sky and Anabel's horror was profound as they passed gibbets carrying human remains which swung and jerked in the breeze, hanging near the spot where their crimes had been committed.

"So many!" she exclaimed. "Can there be so much violence here?"

The Viscount smiled. "It is almost obligatory to be robbed on the Heath. Maybe tonight we shall be lucky though."

Her nerves were stretched to the tearing point when the coach was dragged to a sudden halt and a man shouted, "Hold hard, there, or I shoot!"

"Damnation!" hissed Ryder between his teeth.

Then the coach door was thrown open and a hand holding a large pistol was pointed straight at Anabel's head.

"Now then, sir and madam, hand over your val'ables peaceful like and the lady won't get hurt."

Anabel's heart pounded at the sight of the dark pistol muzzle. Anyone receiving a shot from such a weapon must die. The man was thickset, wearing a coat of frieze. A hat was dragged down over his ears and most of his face was concealed by a black cloth.

The Viscount remained calm as he thrust a hand into his pocket. Anabel held her breath, wondering if he meant to draw a weapon, and she saw the highwayman's eyes glitter. But Ryder, his face expressionless, produced a purse and tossed it to the robber who caught it neatly. "Now your watch, sir."

Slowly his lordship handed over his watch and chain to the man who stuffed them into his pocket. "Thankee kindly, sir. And now for the lady."

"Leave her!" commanded the Viscount. "She is but a poor serving girl whom I befriended."

"That so?" The robber regarded Anabel with interest. "Tain't often a gentry cove in a crested carriage sees fit to help a poor maid. I wonder why..."

Anabel set her lips. She must not antagonize him. If he took her possessions she would be utterly lost.

"Now then, miss, even a serving girl can't journey without a penny. Hand over what you've got."

With trembling fingers Anabel withdrew her purse from her skirt pocket and gave it to the man. With a deft hand he opened it and glanced inside. He let out a long whistle. "Goldfinches! What manner of serving wench be you then? Where there's guineas there may be more. Step down and be quick about it," he said roughly, accompanying his order with a dig of the pistol.

Anabel climbed out of the coach and saw another highwayman, mounted and holding the bridle of a second horse, covering the postilions with a long-barreled pistol. She heard the Viscount and his valet obey an instruction to descend.

The robber glared at her, his eyes merciless. "I'm giving you a few seconds to think, then I shall search you."

"I thought gentlemen of the road left poor folk alone," commented Ryder.

The man grunted. "Pickin's is poor now what with folk sending their bank notes in two halves and the new mail coaches with guards."

His eyes were slate hard as Anabel stood completely still, willing him to go; praying that a coach or riders would arrive to disturb them.

But the only sound was the soughing of the wind and the man stabbed his gun in the direction of her head and snarled. "I'll wait no longer."

Involuntarily Anabel stepped back, her hands clasped. Ryder moved and the robber put the cold metal barrel to Anabel's forehead. "Stay by the coach or the woman gets the barking iron." With a practiced movement his hand was through the opening of her cloak and tearing at her bodice. She gave a cry of revulsion, but dared not move. Then the thick fingers found the leather pouch which hung by a thong between her breasts.

"Women always choose the same place," leered the highwayman. "Will you take it off or shall I?"

Anabel reached behind her head and untied the leather with shaking fingers. She heard the Viscount give a smothered curse, but his rage was as nothing compared with Anabel's as the man opened the bag with his teeth and slid the contents into his palm. Even in the shadows of clouds and trees the gems gleamed with a fire no art could imitate.

The robber gasped at the sight of the necklace of diamonds, emerald eardrops and brooch, the rings and the gold watch. "Serving wench, eh? What service did you give then?"

He gave a lewd chuckle and Anabel felt her body flame with fury. In his dirty hand the man held her future; her escape from the loathed Miles and his family.

The robber grinned. "You never got these by playing servant, I'll be bound."

"Tongue-pad!" The growl came from his companion. "Bag the swag before someone comes to cry beef on us!"

As he spoke the first thief was tipping the contents of his palm back into the bag and the criticism caused him to make an impatient movement which sent the largest of the rings rolling from his hand to land in a patch of mud. He blinked in exasperation. "Pick it up," he ordered Anabel. "Nice and easy now. No quick moves."

Anabel bent for the ring. With a lightning movement she grabbed a handful of the glutinous slime and, throwing herself to one side, slapped it into the robber's face. The Viscount leapt forward. A shot from the man guarding the postilions whistled past them and the one with the jewels aimed his pistol at Ryder who was only feet away. Anabel launched herself from the mud to catch the highwayman's arm and a bullet passed the Viscount to bury itself in the wood of the coach.

She grabbed at her leather pouch and the man

gave a despairing look about him as his companion yelled an oath and galloped past. The first man seized his own saddle and heaved himself into it, disappearing into the trees, but leaving the jewels behind.

"Hell take him," said the Viscount. "I liked that watch."

The postilions quieted the frightened horses and the Viscount gave Anabel a sardonic look.

"My dear Miss Hyde, I would not have thought it possible that anyone—least of all a female—could have afforded me so much amusement and interest. I am exceedingly curious to know how you came by those gems." He retrieved the ring from the mud and handed it to her. "I fear it is dirty, but will soon clean up. Pray, add it to your other—er—acquisitions. Truly, I never visualized myself as having something in common with a highwayman, but I share his wonder as to why you are carrying those jewels. What have you been about, Miss Hyde?"

His mocking laugh splintered her tension into rage. She leapt at him, hands flailing, nails ready to rake his grinning countenance, but he side-stepped easily and grabbed her wrists, holding them in a grip of steel as she twisted and writhed. Another laugh maddened her and she kicked at his booted legs. This seemed to afford him even more gratification. He drew her close and stared into her wide eyes. "Miss Hyde, I beg, no, I insist, that you act with more decorum. The servants are agog with astonishment. It would be entertaining for them—for me also—if you forced me to teach you a lesson as I did before, but if you do not calm yourself, I assure you..."

Hatred whipped through her as she quivered in his grasp, then stopped struggling. He did not release her at once, but gazed deep into her gold-flecked eyes, his face holding an expression she could not fathom. Then he loosened his hold and they climbed into the carriage and resumed the journey.

Four

FOR THE BEST PART OF A MILE no one spoke. Cooper gazed steadfastly from one window and the Viscount from the other. Anabel, between the two, clutched her torn bodice with muddy fingers, wondering desperately how she would cope in London without her precious store of guineas. She ached to loose tears of frustration and shock, but held back. Not for worlds would she allow the hateful man beside her to gain further cause for teasing her.

Ryder spoke first. "We shall soon reach Brentford, Miss Hyde, where you may make yourself presentable."

Anabel longed to tell him to go to the devil and take his suggestion with him, but prudence cautioned her that her problems were severe enough without the disadvantage of walking the street in a ripped gown. Her face colored as she recalled the way she had sprung at the Viscount, forgetting that she would present him with a view of her lace-trimmed bodice and the slight curve of her breasts. Her agitation increased with the shameful realization that she wished she had a more feminine form, that she was not quite so thin.

At the Pigeons Inn, Brentford, the landlord and his wife received her sympathetically when they heard of the brutal attack upon milord's sister. In a private room the mud was sponged away and a maid stitched her gown. Then Anabel combed her hair and secured it in a coil at the nape of her neck.

She descended the stairs with the innkeeper's wife, who announced loudly, "Here she is, my lord. I should take her to see a physician. There's no knowing what such a shock can do to your sister's nerves."

The Viscount, who was at the foot of the stairs, turned with a look of fury. Anabel almost shrank before she realized that she was not the cause. Talking to Lord Ryder was a man of a type she had never before seen. His silk waistcoat matched his pink-and-white-striped stockings, doeskin breeches moulded his legs and his cutaway coat was a marvel of deep purple velvet. Falls of lace adorned his sleeves and neck and the entire outfit was embellished with knots of pink and purple ribbons and silver buckles. He had looked round sharply at the woman's words and now he slowly lifted a quizzing glass on a black silk ribbon, holding it up and rendering one eye enormous. He swept Anabel a low bow which gave her the opportunity to view his high white wig from another angle.

"Pray, introduce me, Ryder. I vow I have never had the honor of meeting your—sister."

The man's thin, rouged mouth smiled and Ryder looked vexed as he said, "May I present Lord Elliot. Miss Hyde, as you well know, is not my sister. She is a traveler who suffered a mishap and I have had the good fortune to be able to help her."

Anabel curtsied, thanking heaven that the sewing maid was skilled, and Lord Elliot's pale eyes flickered over her. "The roads are dreadful, are they not, Miss Hyde? Was your carriage overset? Such weather as we have been having! I never travel far from London, you know. I have not visited my country estates for years."

Anabel was hard put not to stare as Lord Elliot, who chattered like her aunt's friends, astonished her further by producing a snowy lace-trimmed handkerchief which he waved elegantly, releasing a strong perfume, before he touched it to his nose.

Lord Ryder bowed in Anabel's direction. "Shall we proceed, ma'am? Your—relatives will be anxious."

Lord Elliot flicked her with malicious eyes as a woman descended the stairs, laid a proprietory hand on his arm, and dropped a small curtsey. She was far below him in status, her clothes gaudy, her wig curled and adorned to excess, her face painted without skill.

Anabel gave her a cool nod and the Viscount ignored her as he took Anabel's elbow and steered her ungently to the door.

Lord Elliot's effeminate tones floated after them. "Egad, that's a new one. Sister, eh? I must try it sometime, though not with you, my dear. I must discover where he found the woman. Not to my taste, but exceeding genteel."

Anabel kept her head high as the Viscount

handed her into his carriage. "How did that—creature know I was not your sister?"

"I have the ill luck to be distantly related to him," the Viscount grated. "Evil-minded fop that he is! What a misfortune that he should have seen you."

Anabel shrugged, though her stomach felt knotted. "What does it matter? I shall not be moving in his circle."

"True, madam! In fact, I wonder in what circle you do intend to move. Your gowns scarce match your jewels."

"I was wondering how long it would take for you to bring those up!" flared Anabel. "I assure you, sir, they are not dishonestly come by!"

"Did I suggest they were?"

"You implied it! Your mention of my garments...in what others could I have run away?" She bit off the admission that she had no better ones. Her aunt's policy had been to keep her poorly dressed, presumably so that her promises of rich garb to come would be an added lure.

She said coldly, "The jewels belonged to my parents."

Ignoring his lifted brows she stared ahead. And I removed them from Drusilla's jewel case as she slept, her thoughts ran on. She has had them on a "short" loan which has extended several years.

Anabel shivered as she remembered creeping into Drusilla's room, her heart pounding at every creak of the ancient floor. She left her farewell note in place of the diamonds, knowing that it would not be discovered until Drusilla rose at her customary late hour and sent for her usual opulent adornments.

She was reminded of her debts and turned to Ryder. "What is your direction, my lord?"

"For what purpose?"

"So that I may send you the cost of my lodging."

"Pray accept it with my grateful thanks for saving my life," said the Viscount softly.

Anabel stiffened. "I daresay that had I not been with you you would have behaved in a more aggressive manner."

"That is undoubtedly true. I keep a loaded pistol in the carriage."

"You would have shot the man?"

"Most certainly."

"And not for the first time, I'll wager."

"You are correct, madam. I have saved the hangman a task on previous occasions."

"In other words I was a handicap to you. I did not insist on traveling with you. I was prepared to ride in the basket."

The Viscount's voice grew more even. "Miss Hyde, you are as determined to quarrel with me as I am to avoid it. I have had a very trying time over the past few days. My only wish now is..."

"To arrive at your precious rout in good time," finished Anabel.

"My child, you should not be so rude."

"I am not your anything, as I have told you. And you are not so much older than I."

"I am but a youth of two and thirty," sighed the Viscount, "but more ancient in wisdom than you by far." He raised his voice as Anabel began to protest. "Spare me, madam, and listen to me. I assume you have no ready money left."

Anabel remained mute.

"I shall take your silence as affirmation," said Lord Ryder calmly. "Therefore," he continued, drawing a purse from his pocket, "I propose to make you a small loan."

Anabel stared. "You gave your purse to that villain."

"Alas, madam, you are an innocent in the ways of the sinful world. I travel always with two purses. One for the gentlemen of the road and one for myself. Mine, I am happy to say, is always better supplied with gold."

Tears of fury stung the backs of Anabel's eyes. She said with contempt icing her voice, "I shall take no more from you, sir."

His lordship's humor died as with equal coolness he returned, "Indeed, you must. A moment's thought will convince you that you cannot arrive in London tonight with no place to sleep and no money."

Cooper broke his silence. "Oh, Miss Hyde, please take a loan. His lordship's right and he won't miss the money."

The last words caused Anabel to clench her teeth as she forced open her hand. "I shall repay you," she swore.

The Viscount pressed two guineas into her palm; then the carriage was paying its way through the tolls into the city and Anabel's senses were assailed by the sights, sounds and smells of London.

They stopped and Lord Ryder descended. "This is Bond Street where you will be able to obtain lodging over one of the shops. Thank you for your company."

Anabel flushed slightly. She had not been gracious to the Viscount. Another man might have taken extreme advantage of her ignorance.

The Viscount, watching her with an enigmatic expression, said, "I trust you are not going to offer me gratitude. Believe me, I owe you far more than I can express. You have enlivened what might have been one of the most tedious episodes of my life."

She stared into his eyes, feeling her dislike of his arrogance grip her. "How fortunate for you that I chose yesterday to escape from my bondage."

"I do so agree. You have made my stay with the unspeakable Bulmores almost a bearable memory."

Cooper appeared with her bundle of clothes. She took it and the valet held open the chaise door for his master who bowed and lifted Anabel's cold hand in his. He bent and kissed her fingers. "Farewell, Miss Hyde."

She stared down at the brown head; then he rose and stepped lightly into his carriage. Cooper followed him.

"Your direction, my lord," recalled Anabel. "You did not give it to me..."

"It is of no matter. Pray accept the money with my thanks."

Then the door was closed and the carriage

bowled away, quickly lost to sight among other elegant equipages.

Her fingers squeezed the guineas so tightly that they dug into her fingers. She restrained her impulse to hurl them after the departing Viscount. She would find him and repay him, she vowed, though she would not see him herself. She would find a messenger. Never again would she lay herself open to his biting sarcasm.

She looked about her and felt devoutly thankful that she had held on to the money. She was the target for dozens of eyes. In the fading daylight there were many who found Bond Street a place to linger in the gleam of lamps from the shop windows. Carriages rattled over the cobbles taking richly clad folk to their first engagement of the night and two untidy footmen leaned against open doors as their employers were lost to view.

A ballad singer attempted to make himself heard over the cry of a tripe seller and the loudly expressed invitations of shopkeepers to inspect their wares. Washerwomen delivered bundles and a cow mooed as she was led to her byre after a day spent grazing outside the city.

A filthy beggar clawed at Anabel's arm. "Spare a coin, miss. I'm starvin'."

Anabel's eyes widened in sympathy. "I wish I could," she said gently, "but I have nothing to give."

Two guineas and a handful of jewels only lay between her and destitution, but the beggar caught the scent of compassion and pulled at her sleeve, begging piteously.

Two women gave raucous laughs and screamed insults at him before advancing upon him. He released his hold and scurried away, his rags flapping in the cold breeze.

Anabel was torn between relief and anger at the women's callous behavior. They stayed to stare at her. The younger, a girl of about Anabel's age, dressed in tawdry satin and lace and showing a good deal of striped-stockinged leg, grinned. Her teeth were chipped and brown, her eyes speculative. "Well, you're a thin-gut, ain't you," she remarked. "What they been feedin' you? Air puddin'?"

Her witticism was received with applause by the onlookers and an apprentice drew near and dug the girl in the ribs. "Pretty bobbish tonight, eh, Moll!"

Moll shook him off. "I ain't for the likes o' a dandyprat like you, so keep your daddles to yourself."

The apprentice's reply was cut off as a large hand landed a blow on his ear and his master dragged him back to his silk-bag shop while Moll sent a stream of indelicate advice after him.

"Now then, Moll," said the other woman. Deceived by her moderate tones, Anabel turned to her. She felt even more repelled. The woman was much older, garbed in a velvet gown, bedecked with gems, and exuding an air of corruption.

She spoke again and Anabel shuddered at the treacly tones and wrinkled, painted face. "I can see you're fresh up from the country and by the looks of you I make a guess you need a bit of help.

Come along o' Moll and me and we'll take you to a nice bob-ken where you can eat and close your peepers tonight."

She took Anabel's arm in a strong grip and Moll slid an arm about her waist. The heavy odor of unwashed skin overlaid with musk almost over-powered Anabel's senses. Lord Ryder had put her down in a spot where he must have known she would be accosted, embarrassed and frightened. She appreciated her very real danger as a burly man in a long coat, greasy hat and high boots sidled towards them.

"Havin' trouble, Mother Eve? Don't the little ladybird approve of you helpin' her?"

Anabel took a deep breath. Surely in the heart of London it must be possible to call for the assistance of some respectable person. She dug her heels hard into the pavement. "Leave me—all of you! I require nothing of you."

The three exploded with mirth and when Anabel tried to catch the eye of a passing footman he glanced at the burly man and hurried on.

The man put a broken-nailed finger beneath Anabel's chin. "Now you go along with Mother Eve, miss..."

He got no further as a fourth person entered the conversation. "Up to your tricks again?"

Anabel looked at the speaker. She was mature, dressed in sober brown with only a gold chain for adornment and a hat with a single feather.

"Oh, pray, ma'am, will you tell these people...?"

"Ma'am. That's a good 'un!" Moll doubled up in shrieking glee.

"Pay no heed, dearie," said the woman in brown. She turned to Mother Eve. "Let her go or I scream for the Watch."

Mother Eve's vociferous directions to the Watch were many and varied, but she loosened her hold enough to allow Anabel to slip away and stand close to her rescuer. Mother Eve ended with a dissertation on the origins and probable ending of the woman she addressed as Kitty Prowse; then jerking her head at Moll and the man, she stalked off into the night, followed by her two accomplices.

Anabel was overwhelmingly grateful. "I do not know how to thank you. I did not know that London would be so . . . so . . ." Her voice cracked as the past two days merged into a ghastly whole and the woman's face creased in sympathetic lines.

"Ah, it's too bad. An angelic like yourself has no right to be wandering abroad at night. Where's your folks?"

"I...I have none."

"No folks—and nowhere to go?"

Anabel shook her head. "I have some money— a little," she confided. "All I require is a respectable lodging where I can live until I begin to earn."

"Well, if that isn't a miracle!" declared the woman. "Trust Kitty Prowse, my dear. I know of a young gentleman who just got married and took his bride to live in Bethnal Green and I can take you to the very place they left empty only yesterday. Good rooms over a china shop in this street."

Anabel looked doubtful and the woman laughed pleasantly. "You'll meet bad 'uns like Mother Eve everywhere. I promise you the lodgings're all right for you. Clean, with fine rugs and as comfy a bed as you can get."

Anabel ached to rest after the jolting hours in the coach. She took a step in the direction the woman pointed, then hesitated. Kitty Prowse smiled again. "Quite right to be wary, but I'm only asking you to look. The shop's open and the owners there. They live at the back. How can you come to harm just looking?"

The sky was now quite dark and more women of doubtful status were appearing. "How do you know so much about the rooms?" she asked.

"Kitty Prowse knows most things about these parts. Mrs. Small—that's the china shop lady—trusts me enough to ask me to find her a new tenant. She can't be doing with families with young 'uns on account of having to go through the shop to reach the stairs. She'll like you."

As Mrs. Prowse chattered she reached for Anabel's bundle which the girl relinquished, conscious more than ever of her weariness. She followed the woman along Bond Street and into a shop which was glowing with light and filled from floor to ceiling with every conceivable porcelain object.

Moments later Anabel was conducted into rooms above the shop. There were three including a kitchen, furnished with unmatching, but pleasing pieces. It looked more appealing than any place she had seen for a long time.

Mrs. Small coughed. "Of course, miss, I don't usually let my rooms to unmarried ladies. I prefer gentlemen—they're nearly always out—but seeing as how..."

Kitty Prowse threw the woman a look which Anabel's brain was too tired to interpret and Mrs. Small gave another small cough. "My terms are six pounds a year, coals and two tallow candles a week supplied, payable in advance monthly."

Anabel nodded and pulled out a guinea which Mrs. Small bit. She nodded. "That's all right then. I'll bring your change later. The shopboy will carry up some sticks and coal and start you a fire."

Anabel was left looking at Kitty Prowse who said, "Shall I come back tomorrow?"

"Tomorrow...?"

"I can put you in the way of doing things."

"Oh, yes, thank you..."

Kitty left and Anabel dropped her bundle on the drop-leaf table and looked for water. The jug was empty and she had no idea where to fill it. She answered a tap on the door and found Mrs. Small with a jug of milk and a loaf and cheese. A boy walked past with a filled crock of water and the means to make a fire.

The small kindnesses almost made Anabel weep. She ate a morsel of supper, washed herself, and settled into an unexpectedly luxurious feather bed, leaving open the door to watch the leaping flames from the parlor fire.

During the night she was disturbed by the sounds of the city which seemed never to rest, as carriages rattled over the cobbles, the watchman cried the hour, and linkboys shouted for custom. Laughter and shouts fractured the air, but Anabel's body returned each time to the rest it craved and daylight found her refreshed.

As she lay puzzled for a moment by her surroundings she was surprised to find that she wondered if Lord Ryder had enjoyed the rout. She hoped it had proved unendurably tedious; then her savagery gave way to humiliation as she recalled that but for his insistence on lending her money she might have found herself a helpless prey to Mother Eve.

Well, since money was all she could repay, then money he should have.

The empty kitchen shelves bewildered her. All her life she had been accustomed to the appearance of food at set times and the clearing of it by servants. She tore off a piece of the bread and chewed it, washing it down with the rest of the milk, before she drew the curtains and looked down. Grubby girls were scrubbing steps, yawning apprentices opening shutters of shops, and early street traders beginning to shout their wares. A herb seller carried baskets of parsley and thyme, savory and sorrel and Anabel's mouth watered at the idea of mutton with herb sauce. A girl caught sight of her and held up a rosy apple, breathing on it and polishing it on her print kerchief.

Mrs. Small was full of good advice. She sold tea in the shop with the china and sent her shopman to carry a basket loaned for provisions. Anabel walked the noise-drenched London streets and for the first time purchased her own food. At the butcher's she failed completely to identify the cuts of meat in their raw state, but her need to conserve money made her so reluctant to buy too much that the butcher, in the blue coat and apron of his trade, was brought from his original demand of nine-pence a pound for mutton to the legitimate sixpence.

"I took you for a jilly greenhorn," said the shopman, "but you beat him down fine and proper."

Anabel was a fast learner and soon returned with her meat, vegetables, herbs, bread and a bag of sugar-covered queen cakes. Also a quart of ale after the shopman advised her that no one who wanted to reach old age ever drank Thames water. He also reminded her she needed sulfur matches and a tinderbox.

Back in her rooms Anabel faced the fact that she had never been confronted with raw meat and expected to render it eatable, but she borrowed a cookbook from Mrs. Small and at one o'clock dined with a sense of achievement unimpaired by mutton scorched round the edges and vegetables somewhat raw. As she ate a cake and drank ale she felt satisfied with her beginnings.

After tidying, she counted her coins. She called at a tap on the door and Kitty Prowse walked in and consented to take a dish of tea.

"Mrs. Small says you've been managing fine, though it's plain to see you're not used to doing for yourself."

"No," agreed Anabel. "I was wondering—hoping you might put me in the way of earning a living."

Kitty wrinkled her brow. "What can you do?"

"My chief skill lies in painting."

"Oh! Well, I daresay I can find something.

There's always folk wanting inn signs, trade cards and the like. And some of the merchants' womenfolk like to have their likenesses taken. But that might take time. Perhaps if you need money now you've got something you can sell or pawn. Maybe a bauble you've picked up somewhere."

There was a significance in her voice and Anabel's doubts and uncertainties were revived. "Such as what?"

"Oh, I don't know." Kitty shrugged. "It's plain you're from gentlefolk. I thought you might have a ring, or a necklace..."

Anabel threw Kitty Prowse a look which halted her. She had made an exceedingly clever guess at the contents of the leather pouch. She gave the woman a hard look. Was she an accomplice of the robbers? Was this whole offer of help a ruse to complete the work they left unfinished?

All her fragile self-sufficiency dissolved and she felt herself to be ignorantly vulnerable in a harsh world.

Five

KITTY BROKE the uncomfortable silence. "Don't you trust me?"

"You were acquainted with that awful creature—Mother Eve," said Anabel.

"Oh, is that it?" Kitty laughed. "Of course I know her. Everyone who lives in the same bit of London has to be on terms with their neighbors. But you can trust me. You have my Bible oath on't."

Anabel wondered how long it had been since Kitty handled a Bible—or if she ever had, but she had to get help from someone.

Mrs. Small gave Kitty a good character and later that day Anabel, Kitty and a burly shopman walked to the nearest respectable pawnbroker.

Anabel chose to venture alone into the dark shop. An old man shuffled forward and poked the two diamond rings, the emerald brooch and eardrops with an exploratory finger before examining them with an eyeglass.

"These come by honestly?" he growled.

Anabel's chin went up. "They are mine."

He gave her a sharp look and Anabel's heart twisted to watch him as he fingered her mother's gems. "Come down in the world, have you? Or is it your mistress? She been playing too deep at Hazard?"

Anabel remained silent and the pawnbroker said, "I can lend you twenty-six pounds on these."

"Is that all? They are worth double!"

"You won't get a better price if you comb London. I'm not one to cheat. Who sent you here, anyway?"

"A woman—Kitty Prowse."

He nodded. "She'll tell you I don't cheat."

Anabel accepted the man's offer. He tied labels to her jewels and Anabel tucked the tickets into her pocket and left the shop. The money would keep her while she waited to earn.

On the way home she purchased more painting materials and some pretty stuff for new gowns. She ventured an apology to Kitty for doubting her, but Kitty only laughed.

"I'd have thought you a regular whop-straw if you hadn't been careful."

Now that she felt more confident the noise impinged on Anabel's consciousness and between the street criers, beggars, shrieking children darting among the carriages and horses, the shouts of coachmen and grooms, she wondered how anyone managed to pursue a levelheaded existence.

In Oxford Street she was looking into the shop windows when, through the leaded panes of a goldsmith's shop, she saw her cousin Miles talking earnestly to the proprietor.

All her complacency fled as she ducked out of sight, then began to speed along the road.

Kitty kept up breathlessly, "You look as if you've seen a ghost!"

The shopman glared about him, "I'll not let anyone hurt you, miss."

"There is a man," gabbled Anabel, "he musn't see me—I shall be utterly lost..."

Kitty dragged Anabel's hood over her head and the three of them almost ran the length of Oxford Street and were quickly back at the china shop, where Anabel felt a measure of safety.

But she realized that she could not risk trips out and Kitty agreed to pass around the trade cards which Anabel proposed painting.

"If that man—the one who must not see me—goes to the pawnbroker—he will recognize the jewels," she said, as Kitty was preparing to leave.

Her new friend gave a sharp cry of derision. "If he talked he knows he'd never get trade from anyone round these parts. You've nothing to fear from him."

She left and Anabel sorted through her paint box. The rain had not penetrated her pots of color and she sharpened her drawing pencils. She was ready to begin work and felt a deep sense of satisfaction that she had managed without the help of the insufferable Lord Ryder. As the thought sprang into her mind she admitted that he had not been far from her memory. She could easily visualize his sardonic face, set so early into lines induced by his dissolute existence. Well, he would trouble her no more and she could pay her debt.

She emptied her coins onto the table and, fetching a piece of paper, made out a reckoning. She drew up a proper bill, receipted it and put it into a fold of paper with the money, sealing the package with wax and imprinting it deeply with her thumb, as if to emphasize the point.

As she finished there was a scuffle outside her door. She opened it to find two girls of about eighteen. One shuffled her feet and giggled, while the other looked sleepy and full of sulks.

The sulky one spoke. "Is it right you do drawin's?"

Anabel's heart pounded at the idea that she was about to earn money for the first time—and by her own skill.

The girls entered and she looked closely at them, taking in their gowns of satin, their extravagantly dressed hair, their painted faces, and realized with a shock that they were women of the street. It was an even greater shock to accept that she must not object to becoming, as it were, a servant to them. If she was to be professional she must accept all comers.

The giggly girl, who announced herself as Laughing Dorcas, sat first. Anabel had to make three beginnings before her hand steadied; then she lost herself in her work and, after sketching a likeness, mixed paints. In less than an hour she had a prettily tinted watercolor which she called Dorcas to view. The girl giggled, "Won't my man laugh when I show him. It's ever so sweet, miss."

Anabel looked at the sulky one who had sprawled in an easy chair, alternately sighing and dozing.

She rose and came slowly to look. "Not much color, is there? Bit washed out, if you ask me."

Anabel motioned the girl to the sitter's chair.

Again she began to draw, but this time she was quicker. She was learning fast and mixed the color with a heavy hand, washing in the girl's bright gown with acid yellow and her many ribbons with deep colors which never graced a rainbow. The lips were pure vermilion and the dark hair deep black, highlighted so abruptly that the curls appeared oiled.

Sulky-face looked and was transformed. "It's lovely. Cor, I never thought you could paint like that!"

Neither did I, reflected Anabel as the girl turned to her friend, exulting, "Everyone will say Fighting Bet has the best likeness."

Fighting Bet?

"How did you learn of me," she asked, and Anabel was not surprised to know that Kitty Prowse had sent them.

"I'll admit I was tired to death," confessed Bet. "I been workin' all night"—Anabel almost flinched—"but Mrs. Prowse said you was in real bad trouble. Who done it to you, miss?"

Anabel realized that Bet's only interpretation of trouble was the carrying of an inconvenient child and all her efforts could not prevent her blush.

"Nobody done—did anything, Bet. I...I need to stay out of sight, that is all."

Bet touched a finger to her nose. "'Nuff said. Trust us to keep mumchance."

Laughing Dorcas's wistful frown belied her name and Anabel said quickly, "Dorcas, I see now that you are prettier than I have made you."

She began to add color to her first portrait and soothed Bet's return of sulks to explain that she must produce good work as an advertisement, an argument the girl accepted.

Anabel was putting the finishing strokes to the painting when there was a knock.

She called absently, "Please enter," and Lord Ryder stepped into the room.

He was taller than she remembered and more muscular. And her mind had obliterated the way he could smile so that the lines of his face were smoothed out and his eyes rendered warm.

An apparently lazy gaze swept over the room as he took in the scene and gave her a look which brought her hammering heart to greater speed.

"My *dear* Miss Hyde," he said, sauntering towards her.

Anabel retrieved a dropped brush and placed it, handle down, in a waterpot as Lord Ryder peered over her shoulder.

As he contemplated the painting she stifled an urge to protest that she could do better. If the noble Viscount did not like her work he could go hang. It was her living, not his.

She had kept her eyes downcast and was amazed when he dropped a nosegay of wild flowers into the water jar. "For you, Miss Hyde. I thought you might be missing the countryside."

Anabel recognized the tiny speedwell, the yellow-starred aconite and the paler yellow of daffodils. There were snowdrops too and for an instant she was carried back to her childhood beyond the Harcourt Manor days, when she and Papa had walked out and returned with flowers for her ailing mother. She blinked back stinging tears and managed to utter a strangled word of thanks. Perhaps his lordship was kind, after all.

Then, with one of the strokes which could demolish her, he lifted his gold-knobbed cane and touched the still damp paper pinned to the drawing board.

"How splendid! What vibrant color! Never have I seen a watercolor drawing more vividly executed!"

There could be no doubt that he was as aware as she that the art called for the softest-hued washes and she almost pierced her palms with her nails as she clenched her fists.

She was saved from replying by Bet who had automatically preened herself in professional fashion at the sight of a gentleman. "Lovely, ain't it, sir? And what d'you think o' mine?"

Lord Ryder studied the even more garish result of Anabel's portrait of Fighting Bet. "Good God, I find it incredible!"

"Thank you, sir," beamed the delighted girl.

Bet and Dorcas fished florins from their pockets and handed them to Anabel. "We was told it was a fair price," explained Bet.

Then they took their portraits and, promising not to smudge them, departed with noisy clatter and chatter down the stairs.

There was a short silence. Anabel said, "Thank you for the flowers. It was a kind thought."

"Not at all. I was delighted to buy them. They gave me the chance of helping a woman who swore

87

she had a lame husband and twelve hungry children, though for my part I scarce think she has had time to prove so fruitful. However, if she had begun procreation at the age of eight she may be telling the truth. Who can tell how the lower orders run their lives?"

He had been wandering round the room, prodding the chairs and rugs with his cane and Anabel snapped, "Those same lower orders have given me considerable help. I could not have managed without them. It is little enough that you...!"

Lord Ryder swung round, his blue eyes alight with malicious humor. Anabel immediately bit off her words and he looked disappointed.

"Pray, continue, Miss Hyde."

Anabel asked shortly, "How did you find me?"

His lordship grinned and dissembled. "It was not too difficult. May I sit down?"

"Oh, do! You will, anyway."

"How inhospitable. I hoped you might offer me a dish of tea."

"You hoped nothing of the sort! Have you ever drunk tea in your life?"

"Er, no, I must confess—but there must always be a first time."

"Will you stop tormenting me! And if it was so easy to find me then others will do so. I should not have come to London. I did not know it could be so...so parochial."

Lord Ryder gave a shout of mirth. "London! Parochial! I knew I was right to visit you. Life near you is ever diverting."

"How thankful I am to have amused you, sir.

And now perhaps you will go and leave me to my packing."

"Easy there." Lord Ryder crossed one booted leg over the other. "You will not be betrayed. During my perambulations I met a woman named Kitty Prowse. She knows who I am—I am not without a certain fame, Miss Hyde—and asked me to tell you that she has passed word around that your secret must be kept."

"Is that possible?"

"London is a city of surprises. You will be safe— unless you venture forth carelessly and are seen by your late employers."

Anabel looked sharply at him, wondering how much Kitty Prowse had told him. "You seem quick to trust a woman you do not know."

"Oh, everyone in London is acquainted with Mrs. Prowse. Every gentleman that is," his lordship ended softly.

"Oh!" Anabel's cheeks grew pink as she took in the implication of his reply. "Is Kitty Prowse no better than a dreadful creature called Mother Eve?" she demanded.

"Mother Eve?" His lordship looked amused. "Kitty cannot possibly be compared with her! You are safe with Kitty."

Anabel rose and moved agitatedly about the room. "I begin to find that a mixed consolation."

"You do not look consoled at all," remarked the Viscount.

Anabel's words came in a rush. "Oh, how I entertain you, my lord, in my ignorance. I will admit that Mrs. Prowse has been very kind, but to be beholden to such as she!"

The Viscount frowned. "Well, you will have to put up with it, in exactly the same way you were forced to accept the assistance I was able to render."

A slow smile spread over Anabel's face. She opened her palm and looked down at the florins. "I came by this money through my own efforts. You could not imagine how gratifying that is. I suppose you never will, you being such a fine gentleman, my lord."

She swept him a curtsey as her voice took on the accent of her two sitters.

"A mimic too, by God," breathed the Viscount. "'Pon my soul, madam, if painting fails you could try the boards. Many an actress has married into the nobility."

"Well, how truly wonderful for them." Anabel's face expressed her mockery. "You cannot believe, can you, that I have as little desire to bind myself in matrimony as you have. Perhaps we are nearer in temperament than you suppose."

Lord Ryder dropped his cane and rose. Two long strides brought him close and his hands imprisoned her narrow waist. For a long moment they stared into one another's eyes. Anabel threw back her head. "I cannot stop you, sir, and I would not wish to lower my pride by calling for help."

"Is that so? In some women I would call that an invitation to proceed."

"In the circles in which you appear to move I am not in the least surprised."

Anger flared in his eyes and Anabel registered a hit. She smiled. "You are not so desirous to receive insults as to give them."

His lordship's hands slid slowly down until he imprisoned her hands by her sides. Anabel remained motionless and as he removed his hands suppressed a grimace of triumph. Then she walked to the table and picked up a sealed package. She held it concealed against her skirt as she asked, "Will you answer my question as to your purpose in seeking me out?"

Lord Ryder gave her a deep look. Deliberately he raised his white hand to smother a small yawn. "I was insufferably bored, Miss Hyde. It amounts almost to a disease with me."

The words shattered any reluctance she might have had. She held out her hand. "I pray that this will divert you further, sir. You will find it a true rendering insofar as it lies within my knowledge."

Lord Ryder took the package with lazy hands. At the chink of coins his eyes narrowed and he glanced up at her. She hid her eagerness while he removed the outer wrapping and picked up a slip of paper.

In a bland voice he read: "Item: 106 miles in carriage; £1 11s. 6d. Item: Lodging for one night and part of a day; 10s. 6d. Item: Food on journey; 1s. 6d. Item: Repayment of loan; 2 guineas with 8s. interest."

The Viscount remained staring down at the paper and for a brief moment Anabel felt nervous. She held herself ready for his arguments, or fury, or both. She was half-relieved—half-disappointed when, after counting the coins, he retied the package and slipped it into the pocket of his dark green cloth coat, saying only, "Thank you, Miss Hyde."

He reseated himself, as he remarked conversationally, "It remains cold, does it not? One hopes for the sun when one may stroll in the parks. Have you seen our London parks, Miss Hyde? No? You must take the air some time—in a suitable disguise, of course. I also ride frequently. It does not do to lose one's skill in equestrian arts. You have not yet ridden in London, have you?"

Anabel seethed. What an inane, socializing creature he was. She brushed aside the suspicion that her petulance was due to his calm acceptance of the money. She wondered how he gauged so exactly how to anger her.

With a tremendous effort she answered his question. "I have that joy to come, sir."

Lord Ryder gave her an anxious look. "How unlike yourself you sound. I pray you are not taking a cold. It is as well you did not ride in the coach basket or you might have had lung fever."

To her immense irritation he produced a handkerchief which he sniffed gently. "I am told that Friar's Balsam is an excellent remedy for warding off humors associated with colds, but it is not the smell one wishes to be associated with. I daresay my cedarwood will do almost as well. My valet, an estimable man, becomes distrait if I refuse *all* perfume. So fashionable, you know—so I humor him by using one I consider masculine, though since Brummell has become king of fashion it has grown almost obligatory to dress plainly and use soap rather than scent."

"Indeed! I find your lordship's observations upon society quite fascinating."

"Do you? I should not have thought it."

His glance had flickered over her brown stuff gown over which she had tied a borrowed holland apron.

She rushed to defend herself. "I have not yet had time to make up my new materials."

She wished she had held her tongue as the Viscount looked delighted. He was baiting her and she had jumped headlong into his trap. She sought for something which would pierce his urbanity when she looked up to find him watching her with an intensity of annoyance which shook her. His voice and remarks belied his emotions. She had succeeded in enraging him. She felt satisfaction war with craven fear. Had she gone too far? Would he consider betraying her?

Suddenly she wished he would go. A part of her had rejoiced to see him enter her rooms, yet with all her heart she prayed he would leave her alone. The silence had lasted too long and she felt incapable of breaking it. She was relieved when someone came to her door. She opened it and stood back as two girls pushed and giggled their way into her parlor. They were gowned in tawdry, spangled finery. Their skirts left an unusual amount of leg exhibited. Their shoes were scarlet with high, spangle-dotted heels and silvery buckles.

"You the lady what does the painting?" asked one.

Anabel managed a choked, "Yes."

"Me and my friend, Patty, here, saw what you done for Fighting Bet and Laughing Dorcas. We're opera dancers. Will you do us?"

Anabel nodded as she saw Lord Ryder take up his beribboned eyeglass and hold it toward the girls.

He rose and bowed to Anabel. "I bid you good day, Miss Hyde. I am glad to know you will not starve."

He came close. "One day," he remarked in low tones, "you must explain to me why your late employers are so anxious to keep you—and why you fear them so."

He executed a flourishing bow to the opera dancers. "Happy sitting, ladies!" Then he was gone.

Anabel drew mechanically, keeping her mind on the task in hand. She was disturbed by another caller and found Jacky, the shop apprentice lad, holding an exquisitely pretty white luster vase. "The lord bought this for you," he grinned.

Anabel stared, unable to articulate. Jacky looked uncertain, then placed the vase at her feet and ran downstairs. For an instant her foot itched to kick the vase after him, but she could not shatter so lovely an object. She lifted it, caressed its gleaming surface, then filled it with water and dropped in the nosegay. The admixture of white and delicate color was balm to her senses and she grew even more confused by the conflict within herself.

Benefiting by her lesson learned from Dorcas and Bet she executed the colored drawings of the dancers in variegated colors which would have provoked Lord Ryder to heights of wit. She cursed him silently, biting her lips as she worked. She could only hope that having seen her settled he would leave her alone.

For three days an increasing number of women came to her lodging. She counted the florins incredulously. At this rate she would have no financial worries. She could even contemplate hiring a servant, having concluded that her cooking left much to be desired.

Then Mrs. Small came and shattered Anabel's content. Her pleasant features were screwed into a scowl as she explained that the china shop had always been respectable and no more was she going to allow ladybirds and lightskirts over her threshold. "And Mr. Small is mortified," she finished. "Next thing you know we shall be losing our good trade."

Anabel was contrite. "I did not think! What am I to do? I must live."

Mrs. Small's face relaxed and she sat down as she realized that Anabel would cooperate. "You don't have to mix with the low women. Plenty of merchants would pay to have their wives and daughters painted."

"That is what I hoped, but how do I contact them?"

"Make your trade cards," advised Mrs. Small. "I'll have a word with Kitty Prowse and between us we'll get your custom up to a proper level."

95

The next day found Anabel, without customers, working on pieces of pasteboard on which she announced: "Miss Hyde is skilled in drawing and watercolors and resides above the China Shop of Mr. Small in Bond Street. She will be pleased to take the likenesses of any lady or gentleman who so desires. Moderate terms."

Jacky was despatched to various shops and coffee houses and Anabel set about seeking a maid.

She selected one, Sally Tomkins—"fresh up from the country, ma'am—and I want a taste of town life." She declared herself happy to attend her new mistress from her lodging in a nearby street and Anabel congratulated herself on her ability to manage her own affairs.

Sally was also a nimble seamstress and, after cleaning Anabel's rooms, applied herself to stitching the new materials into gowns.

Six

ANABEL HIRED A HACKNEY to take her shopping, enduring the musty straw-floored coach to lessen any risk of being seen by Miles who might still be in town.

She and Sally called first at a bookshop to consult patterns in the fashion magazines, and after grimacing at the idea of herself mixing paints in snowy muslins, Anabel bought blue poplin, green-and-white-striped damask which could be turned, and muslin for neckerchiefs.

She declined a milliner's offer to sell her many hats and chose a simple straw and bought feathers and ribbons for trimming. She could not resist some silk stockings and two pairs of kid pumps, and she and Sally made their way home by way of sundry food shops where the maid did the marketing.

After a splendid meal of apple and pork pie with nutmeg and celery and an orange cream, Anabel sipped coffee, nibbled gingerbreads and tackled Sally on the subject of her wages, expressing surprise at the girl's apparent lack of interest.

Sally put down the tray and shifted knives and forks needlessly. "I know you'll see me right, miss."

"I cannot think why you are so sure. You do not know me."

Sally offered no reply and Anabel continued. "I may as well be frank—I have no experience in employing servants. What do you usually ask?"

Sally looked relieved. "Five pounds a year and my food."

"It seems so little!"

Sally laughed. "It's enough, honest, miss. Shall I go on with sewing your gowns when I've washed the pots?"

"Yes, please. No, wait a moment. Have you ever met—are you acquainted with a woman named Kitty Prowse?"

"No, miss. I don't know of her."

She picked up the tray and went into the kitchen where Anabel heard her singing softly as she worked. Anabel liked Sally, but continued to feel a little uneasy.

But the necessity to earn a living drove all else from her head. When she ventured into the china shop downstairs she was fascinated by the bustle. Ladies examined china and made purchases and their maids and footmen carried them to waiting carriages. Some customers seemed simply to sit on the small chairs and enjoy a good gossip. Anabel's senses were tantalized by the colors of the gowns and the fragrant perfumes. She found it difficult to conceal incredulity at the number of pockmarked faces, ill concealed by maquillage. Some folk wore wigs and others powdered hair, but most, influenced possibly by the new Powder Tax, had reverted to displaying their own hair.

Suddenly Anabel longed to be part of the world of the *haut ton;* to laugh at the witty essays—even to understand their meaning since they concerned matters outside her experience. One day, she promised herself, I will find my place.

As she and Sally sewed her new gowns the face and form of Ryder came constantly to plague Anabel's memory. She told herself that it was not surprising since he was the only man outside her family with whom she had had prolonged contact; he was certainly the only man who had kissed her—and with such disturbing passion she recalled, her body burning with the memory of her quick response. I hate him, she told herself. I despise him for taking advantage of a helpless woman. But he could have harmed her and he had been merciful. He could have abandoned her and he had protected her. Only while it amused him, she reminded herself fiercely. Once in London he had dumped her with as little ceremony as he would have dealt with a sack of potatoes.

She jabbed savagely at the poplin, managed to prick her finger and only just stopped a blob of blood from staining the cloth.

One sunny morning Anabel was able to put on her new blue gown. She draped a neckerchief round her shoulders, tucking the ends into her bodice, and allowed Sally to dress her hair. The girl had persuaded her to have her pale gold tresses cut and now she drew the shining strands from Anabel's face and secured them with a blue ribbon.

Anabel looked in her mirror and almost believed her maid when she clasped her hands and pronounced her elegant. She decided that she possessed a certain distinction and with that must be satisfied. She tied on a new chintz apron, picked up a lace cap and put it down, unwilling to disarrange her coiffure.

She was kept busy with her new clientele who arrived to be painted in their Sunday finery. Kitty had taken Papa's gold watch to the pawnbroker who had allowed her ten pounds. She could not bring herself to send the gold rings exchanged by her parents. All she had left was the necklace and that she was resolved to keep in case of real emergency.

She was finishing the picture of the stout wife of a cheesemonger when Sally showed someone in. "Pray be seated," Anabel invited, without looking round. "I will not keep you waiting long."

She put the final touches to a scarlet feather which topped an improbably auburn head of hair before she turned to see Lord Ryder, sprawled in the easy chair, a gleam of sardonic humor lighting his eyes.

Anabel was annoyed at the swift gratitude she felt at knowing she looked attractive as she accepted the plaudits of the lady who wheezed out with her picture.

As she cleaned her brushes she asked, "What brings you here, my lord? Have you nothing better to do?"

"How unbusinesslike of you. I have come because I was passing a dull hour in a coffee shop, reading my newspapers which were full of the most tedious happenings, when I chanced to see a trade card propped against a tobacco jar. It is an age since I had my likeness taken and I feel the omission should be repaired."

Anabel glared at him. "Do not be ridiculous, sir. Viscount Ryder should find a painter who works in oils. Something of mine would not do to hang in your gallery of ancestors."

The blues eyes flashed a warning. "I am not accustomed to being labeled ridiculous, madam."

Anabel turned her back to him. "Are you not?" she asked, pointing the sable hairs of a brush with a delicate touch. "That is because you meet only with those who curry favor with you. I am not of their number."

She had scarcely heard him move when he was behind her, his hands gripping her elbows.

"Let me go! How dare you!"

"Apologize!"

"I will not. Leave my rooms! I refuse to paint you!"

With a powerful movement he spun her round to face him. His arms fell to his sides, but she was mesmerized by his baleful stare. "What do you fear, Miss Hyde?"

"Nothing, sir!"

"Nothing? Are you positive? I kissed you once and you did little to prevent me."

Anabel flushed. "You are stronger than I. How can a woman fight a man with such unequal odds against her?"

"I gained the impression that your lips moved under mine in a provocative way—and do not trou-

ble to deny it. I know the difference between re-
pulse and response."

"I believe you! Get out of my lodging and stay
out!"

"I want you to paint me."

"I will not. I shall call a magistrate."

Her threat was empty and they both knew it.
"You will not call for help, Miss Hyde, will you?
You cannot afford to."

She stared at him, enmity whipping through
her. "Very well. You use unfair weapons, my lord.
I will paint you if it is the only way to be rid of
you."

Lord Ryder smiled. "How impolite you are. And
I make no guarantee that I will not return."

He seated himself and stared toward her.

"Be so good as to turn your head," she ordered
distantly. "I shall draw your profile."

"I prefer full face and I am the customer."

She would not demean herself by further argument and pinned a fresh paper to the drawing
board. At first her hand shook as she caught the
intense look in his eyes, but her fury sustained
her and she drew more rapidly than ever before,
dashing down the lines with savagery. She repro-
duced the planes of his face, the harsh peaks and
shadows, blocking in shaded areas with strokes of
soft lead. She lost passage of time and Lord Ryder
maintained perfect muscle control.

At last Anabel threw down her pencils and her
release of tension sent her neck into a painful
spasm. Her effort to conceal the pain gave her face

a severity, a contemptuous appearance to her mouth that Lord Ryder could not miss.

He rose, flexed his shoulders and strolled over to look at the picture. He drew a sharp intake of breath. "So!" he said softly, "you have talent after all."

Anabel gazed at her work. It was the best thing she had ever done and it amazed her.

Slowly he unpinned the picture as Anabel protested without conviction, "I have not yet added color."

"Quite unnecessary. It is finished—as complete as ever it needs to be. My congratulations, madam." Then with deliberation he removed a florin from his pocket and handed it to her.

As she had ached to refuse the loan of his guineas she felt a momentary urge to spurn the florin, but she had earned this money and she took it.

"I also pay my debts in full," observed the Viscount.

Then with a bow he was gone and Anabel sank into the chair still warm from his body and tried to cope with the tumult of emotions which assailed her, breaking through the dam of her defenses, seeking out the hidden places of her mind.

The best thing she had ever done! She went further. It was the only truly good thing she had ever done. She was, she admitted it, merely a competent artist, never destined for greatness. A dry sob escaped her as she contemplated her future. With what would she console her mind—that much vaunted part of herself which she had striven to cultivate?

Why had a man she detested to be the person to inspire her? She paced her room, twisting her hands, her poplin skirt rustling like a winter wind through withered leaves.

How she abominated him—the man who could so quickly pierce her guard. Hate was akin to love! What nonsense her mind was weaving! No man would breach her reserve. She had begun to forge it at the age of fourteen when her cousin began his concentrated persecution, alternating his hair-pulling and tattlemongering with filthy forced kisses, rendering her in a constant state of apprehension.

She could not endure it if everything she had so meticulously built up were to vanish, as surely it would if she admitted her vulnerability toward a man. Especially one who used her as a plaything, to while away a bored hour; a transitory amusement in a despicable mode of life.

She thrust the treacherous ideas away and worked through the days, adding to her store of coins, yet, where previously it had been difficult to prevent Ryder's image from invading her mind, now it was impossible. Her drawing of him had marked more than the paper; it was acid-etched into her brain. It tormented her when awake and permeated her dreams when asleep.

In Harcourt Manor she had scorned to allow her relatives to see her shadowed eyes and pale complexion, induced by their unkindness, and had used her study of ancient recipes found in books in the library to manufacture simple, but effective, cosmetics. She had applied her knowledge of painting to lighten her better points with touches of rose and cream and to conceal faults by the subtle shading of blue. Now she was glad of the lessons she had learned. Lord Ryder should not think he could affect her adversely.

As a week passed with no sign of the Viscount she tried to convince herself she was glad. Then Sally admitted a client who brought a fresh upsurge of anxiety.

She had completed the drawing of two daughters of a corn factor when she looked up to find herself observed by a man she recognized. Memory quickened her heartbeats. He was Lord Ryder's kinsman, Lord Elliot. He who had encountered her posing as Ryder's sister at a common inn.

He strolled forward, his pale hands raising an eyeglass to survey first the portraits, then the giggling girls who became all blushes and confusion. He obviously regarded them as beneath his notice and ignored them till they left.

Anabel began to wash her brushes. "What may I do for you, sir?" she asked, keeping her voice casual.

Perhaps he would not know her. After all, she was prettily gowned, with a new hair style, and carefully applied cosmetics. Her hopes were at once destroyed.

Lord Elliot bowed. "So you are the same girl! I have been wondering ever since I heard of you, though Ryder has, of course, many little friends."

His thin lips parted in a smile, revealing teeth showing signs of decay. She maintained a cool

105

stare into his face, which was coated with heavy white and crimson, then returned to her brushes.

"Have we met, sir?"

Elliot's soft laugh made her shiver inwardly. "Oh, come now, madam! You know perfectly well that we were introduced."

He covered his mouth as he yawned. "I do assure you, I care as little for Ryder's morals as I care for him. My dear cousin may do as he pleases—he always has."

Anabel's face flamed into color. "You insult *me*, sir! My morals are sound."

"Really! Few of us can say as much. Then again, many of us do say so and are not speaking the truth."

Anabel was silent. She would never convince him that she was not engaged in an illicit relationship with Lord Ryder.

He sauntered round the room on green satin shoes with high heels and silver-edged bows. The rest of his attire was extravagantly adorned and Anabel found herself comparing his appearance unfavorably with Ryder's.

She felt a sudden yearning for his presence. He would not allow her to be insulted. But how was she so sure he would defend her honor? Perhaps he had told Elliot of her, with sneers and insinuations. She tried to reassure herself that he would not.

Lord Elliot asked, "Where should I sit?"

As Anabel stared he said, "To have my portrait taken. Why do you think I am here?"

"Is that...that truly your reason for seeking me out?"

"For what other?"

Anabel stammered, "I...I daresay you saw one of my trade cards."

Elliot smiled thinly. "As it happens, my valet is making amorous advances to a serving wench in Ryder's house. Through him I learned of your portrait. I called and was most impressed."

As Anabel continued to stare at him he said, "It is known among the servants that my kinsman conveyed a girl to town and visits her in her apartments."

Anabel burned to think of tattling tongues tearing at her reputation as Elliot continued, "Pray, do not trouble yourself with below-stairs gossip. It may not reach the ears of the society tabbies."

"Your cousin was gallant enough to help me when I became distressed on my journey to London..."

"I lay bets he was!" His lordship continued musingly, "I suppose he was bored—he usually is—and if no other diversion offered...."

"Get out! Leave my home!"

For answer Lord Elliot dusted the seat of the sitter's chair, murmuring, "I hope the taint of trade does not rub off. Now, Miss Hyde, begin your drawing."

"I think you misheard me. I have no intention of..."

"Oh, but you must!" Lord Elliot's voice was not raised, as he settled himself in the chair, but his tone was menacing. "I do so hate to appear

107

threatening, but if you continue to annoy me I may pursue certain inquiries."

Her skin crawled. "Inquiries, sir? Of what nature can you mean?"

Lord Elliot studied his long fingernails. "You have an excellent notion, Miss Hyde. After you have obeyed me, you should purchase a newspaper. Try the *Daily Advertiser,* or perhaps the *Morning Chronicle.*"

A faint smile appeared on his painted face, "Come, Miss Hyde. I am becoming weary. Take up your pencils."

With his sharp features, his cruel mouth and long nails he reminded her of a bird of prey. And she was his victim, transfixed with horror. Yet she would not relinquish her independence easily.

"You threaten me, sir," she said in low tones.

His face set in angry lines. "I am not accustomed to defiance, especially from females. It has become the knowledge of any who can read that a certain lady has left her relatives' home and that her whereabouts are sought."

"There must be many women who..."

"Do not play the fool, madam. There is a description."

"Is the price of your silence a drawing?"

Her voice was contemptuous and color glowed for an instant through the maquillage. "Do not rile me, or I may turn you in to the authorities."

Anabel gave in, picking up her pencils. After several false starts she produced a likeness of Lord Elliot. He came to view it and his eyes slitted with rage. Anabel suddenly saw the drawing from his viewpoint. She had captured him well, but whereas in Ryder she had found a measure of beauty and an unexpected integrity, here lay the ugliness of brutality and an ill-spent life.

"I...I will do another," she began, but Elliot ripped the paper from the retaining pins.

"I shall keep it."

"I drew only what was there." That was wrong and she tried again. "I was angry with you. Give me the chance to try again."

Elliot rolled up the paper with hands which shook a little. He took out two shillings and threw them down so viciously that they fell from the table and rolled on the floor, spinning and clattering.

"Your price, I believe."

He was gone and Anabel heard the tapping of his heels on the stairs. There was an altercation from the foot of the stairs, footsteps and a knock. She admitted Lord Ryder, who looked angry.

"Why was Elliot here? What did he want? Has he touched you—annoyed you in any way?"

All Anabel's pent-up fear rose and burst forth. "How dare you walk in and demand answers to questions which are none of your concern! Mind your own business!"

She should have known better by now. Lord Ryder reached out and, grabbing her wrists, jerked her from the door and kicked it shut. "You will inform me what that vile filth was doing in your rooms."

Anabel twisted and fought. "You are hurting me! Release me, my lord!"

"Damn you! Answer my questions!"

Suddenly she stopped struggling, close to tears, recognizing that her frantic resistance was born partly of her need to withstand the exquisite touch of his hands. Shame overcame her at the impulse of desire which made her ache to press her body to his. She stood passive in his grip, her eyes veiled, and Lord Ryder's touch became gentle as he rubbed her wrists soothingly.

"Why do you provoke me? No other woman…"

He dropped her hands and walked to the window to gaze into the street. "Do you find it noisy here after the peace of Harcourt Manor?"

"The manor was not peaceful to me, sir. I was forever being disturbed in the course of my—duties."

He turned and she traced with her mind the lines of his face, his deeply blue eyes, his mobile lips…."

"I was only drawing Lord Elliot," she said.

He reached into his pocket and drew out a piece torn from a newspaper. "Read this and explain it to me."

"I owe you no explanations."

He thrust the paper into her hand and she read: "Run from the safety of her home and thought to be in London, Miss Harcourt of Harcourt Manor. She is twenty years and tall, being five feet seven inches and slender of build. Her face is unmarked and of pale complexion. Her hair is very fair and her eyes brown. It is feared she may be out of her senses and in moral danger." There followed a description of her clothes. The insert finished: "If any should find the young lady and return her to the bosom of her anxious family they will receive a Reward."

Anabel sat down heavily, feeling intensely weary. She supposed someone must have seen her chasing the London stagecoach. Miles would certainly have overtaken it and questioned the driver and guard.

Lord Ryder's voice was sympathetic. "You are Miss Harcourt, are you not?"

She nodded and he asked, "Why did you lie to me?"

"If you had known I was related to 'the abominable Bulmores' would you not have found a perverse joy in taking me back?"

He looked put out. "Naturally I would not have spoken in those terms if you had informed me that you were a poor relative seeking to escape."

Anabel opened her mouth and closed it again.

"You were about to say...?"

"N...nothing."

"What are the Bulmores to you?"

"Mrs. Bulmore is my late father's sister."

"Have you no other family?"

"None. My father directed in his will that I should be in their charge until I came of age."

"Monstrous! How could he leave you at the mercy of such folk?"

"They had not met since they were young." Anabel's anger flared. "I know he could not have been aware of how unkind she has become."

"Obviously not. It is iniquitous that children

111

without parents can be so completely controlled by unscrupulous relatives."

"You sound genuinely sorry."

"That surprises you?"

"I have had small reason to suppose you compassionate," she flashed, raising quick defenses of aggression against the unruly longings he raised in her.

Lord Ryder's eyes grew cool. "Why does the manor bear your name?"

Anabel said evenly, "It is my ancient family dwelling. My father chose to reside near my mother's birthplace which she loved."

"I see. And the manor…"

"…has been my uncle's for many years," finished Anabel.

His face was dark with fury at her dismissive tone. "And the jewels—to whom did they belong?"

"It is evident that you think I purloined them."

The rapport which she found so disturbing was destroyed and she was glad.

"I would not have used so harsh a term," he said levelly, "but I will not argue with you."

He turned to go and she stared after him, memorizing the set of his shoulders, the length of his booted legs, the way his hair sprang from his head. Perhaps they would not meet again.

"I suppose the man who drove so fast into the inn yard was your uncle," he said, at the door.

"Miles," she corrected. "My uncle suffers from the gout and never travels further than Bath or Bristol. Besides, Miles is forever hankering after

112

London. Any excuse would be enough to make him come."

"Is that so? By the way, do not make any plans to change your address. Elliot has one of his minions watching you. He is in no mind to see an end to the fun. Continue to charm us all, Miss Harcourt, and your secret should be safe for the present."

Seven

A LITTLE DETECTING PROVED THAT there were many people who seemed to have nothing to do but lounge all day in Bond Street, but Anabel could not tell if any had been set to watch her. Why should Lord Elliot spy on her? Was it simply to irritate his cousin, Ryder?

She waited in trepidation after the appearance of the advertisement, but when she was unmolested she began to relax, resisting the unpleasant idea that she was trapped in her rooms as surely as if she inhabited one of His Majesty's jails. But she must submit if she was to remain free from Miles. He would not come here. His vanity was too immense to ask for a drawing by a nonentity. Meanwhile her work was becoming popular and she was kept busy.

Her clients were rising in status, one or two inhabiting the fringes of the *ton* world. Nevertheless she was surprised when, on a day when a March wind was weaving patterns from the clouds, she received a message from Esther, Lady Finch, announcing that she would be with her before noon. The autocratic terms assured Anabel that Lady Finch must be considered nobly born.

The parlor was neat when her ladyship arrived, accompanied by a young woman and escorted by Lord Elliot, whose appearance Anabel found unnerving.

Lady Finch was a dowager who had retained the fashion of high, powdered wig, and was dazzling in an open robe of vivid green taffeta over pink muslin. A purple fur-lined cloak was draped over her shoulders and atop her ringleted hair was a many-feathered hat. She and Lord Elliot in his blue-and-silver-striped waistcoat, yellow nankeen breeches and brown velvet coat looked like two birds of paradise in an inadequate cage.

The young woman was introduced as Miss Pamela Smithson whose portrait Anabel was to take. Anabel felt shocked at her looks. Miss Smithson was about seventeen, though it was difficult to assess her years through the thick coating of dead white paint out of which her eyes peered as if from a mask. She was somewhat plump and was squeezed into stays which must pinch her cruelly. Her gown of white muslin and hat of pink satin with crimson feathers aggravated her clownlike face.

Lady Finch indicated the girl with a long beribboned cane. "I desire you to paint my ward. Elliot tells me you have a certain skill. You must make her handsome, mark you. There is a suitor in Scotland of whom we have hopes. He lives to the far north where one must needs ride horseback, though I thank heaven it is unlikely I shall ever visit him."

As her autocratic voice boomed on, the sick humiliation in the girl's eyes made Anabel wince. "The young man's uncle is in town seeking a suitable bride who will not object to leaving the *haut ton*. He agrees with me that a young lady of such fortune as my ward will be entirely desirable— financially that is. We propose to send a likeness to the man so you must make it pretty enough to insure that he agrees to a betrothal at a distance. Then he cannot back away."

At Miss Smithson's strangled protest her guardian glared. "You have only to look in a mirror to know I am right." She turned to Anabel. "She had the smallpox as a child and it has left her looking very nasty. Still, she is lucky not to have died along with her sisters."

The girl's appearance was further marred by tears which fell over her paint and turned her nose pink. "I would prefer to meet him before we become irrevocably tied."

"Such effrontery from a young gel!"

"But natural," interposed Anabel, forgetting for a moment her humble station.

Lady Finch looked startled before she frowned.

Lord Elliot bowed, "Do you not wish to take the commission, Miss...er, Hyde?"

Anabel could not miss the threat in his voice. How dull his life must be if he took pleasure in tormenting her. As dull as his cousin's! As soon as she was free she would turn her back on such mindless people.

"Shall I paint her as she is?" she asked, "with her cosmetics clearly defined?"

"Paint her as a beauty," ordered Lady Finch.

"Let's entrap the man before he becomes enamored of some Scots wench."

Her brutal vulgarity made Anabel think that there were fates equally evil to being incarcerated in a country mansion with Miles Bulmore and his family. The girl was trembling when she laid a hand on her forehead. "It is difficult to see her face at all, Lady Finch," she said, maintaining a humble tone. "May I remove her paint? I have an idea."

Her ladyship stared. "You will make her pretty, mind you. Well, you can scarcely do worse. Elliot, you will escort me to Oxford Street. I must needs buy muslin for gowns for my ward. The bird-witted laundry maid has torn three beyond repair, damn her eyes!"

As she departed, Miss Smithson muttered angrily, "Those gowns were so old I feared they might drop off and leave me naked. She does not think me worth dressing and is mean with my money."

She sat and permitted Anabel to scrape off the white paint. "Does not your guardian know the danger of using lead paint?" Anabel asked.

The girl shrugged. "I have heard that rumor too. She does not care. If she had done her duty I would not have caught the smallpox and my dear sisters...! She was too busy enjoying herself to insure that we had the inoculation. Now she vows she can scarce bear to look at me."

"And you are using red lead also!" exclaimed Anabel. "My poor child, if you could contrive to fall in love with your Scotsman it might be good for you. He may not allow you to use these cosmetics."

"Then he'd see me as I really am!"

Anabel took a handful of cold cream and massaged the girl's face.

"How delightfully cool. What is it?"

"A mixture I learned from an old Greek recipe. An emulsion of almond oil, spring water and beeswax."

Anabel finished cleaning the skin and looked searchingly at Miss Smithson who flushed. "It is not so bad. There is some pitting and your eyebrows are thin, but not all the blemishes are from the smallpox. Have you been bothered by pimples?"

"All the time! I have no luck at all."

"You must persuade your husband to allow plenty of greenstuffs on the table. Good garden produce is better for the complexion than rich food."

Anabel began to mix creams and lotions, assisted by Sally, then she tied gauze round her client's dark hair. As she applied *pomade à baton*, she talked reassuringly. "If you still wish to paint white I will make up a pot of Briancon chalk in distilled vinegar. It is almost ready. Meanwhile ... starch and rosewater are a good foundation."

She had finished and Sally brushed Miss Smithson's hair, then dressed it in the orderly disorder seen in the fashion magazines, threading a pink ribbon through the curls and securing it with a tiny pearl brooch Miss Smithson removed from her corsage.

Sally held up a looking glass and the girl stared disbelievingly. "It is a miracle! I am so different.

119

I always thought my eyes my best feature and you have drawn attention to them. I might almost be pretty."

"They look as nature intended—almost." Anabel smiled. "I have used a touch of blue above them and green below. The lip salve is of damask roses in beeswax. Nothing there can hurt you."

The girl touched her brows. "How have you darkened them so softly?"

"A judicial use of burnt clove."

"Well! I must have all the preparations for my own use. I will pay whatever you ask."

"By all means, though I will not overcharge you. Add it to the cost of the portrait."

"No!" Miss Smithson took out her purse. "*She* will not pay. Take your fee now."

Anabel drew the portrait swiftly, laying in the color as nearly as possible to the new face she had created. The girl was enchanted. "I shall be proud to send it to Scotland."

"Shall you not mind going now?"

"Oh, I think not. His letters are kind and witty."

"Why were you so upset?"

"Because my portrait would have looked like the painted doll my guardian made me. Now he will notice my eyes and hair. Perhaps he will not mind about the rest."

Anabel felt gratified. Since arriving in London she had been shocked to see so many pox-ruined skins. Now, thanks to Dr. Jenner, her own children would have the new cowpox and be safe.

A spasm twisted her face. What a fool she was! She was not going to marry and bear children. If intimacy with a man was the sordid experience revealed by Miles.... Unbidden came a recollection of vastly different lovemaking. Lord Ryder's lips were hard and clean; his controlled passion quickly evoked response in her.

She started at the sound of Lady Finch's voice on the stairway. Her ladyship and Elliot burst into the room. "Lord, it is unseasonably hot!" Lady Finch wafted air with a lacquered fan. "Have you finished? Good God! What have you done to her?"

She strode to her ward and jerked her face to the light. "What is this? It will not do!"

Anabel needed her ladyship's approbation. "She is prettier," she pointed out.

"Prettier be damned. She must be fashionable."

Miss Smithson, emboldened by her new looks, argued, "I have read that lighter painting is coming into vogue."

"No lady in *my* circle would dare to venture abroad without the heavy use of white."

"I know many who are hideous from lead painting," cried the girl, "and if you interfere I shall write to my suitor in tones which will leave me on your hands."

Lady Finch's face darkened in fuming rage. "Very well, miss. We cannot return home anyway as we are engaged to play whist in less than half an hour." She tossed a florin onto the table. "Keep the picture until later. It is damp."

She stalked out and Miss Smithson threw Anabel a look of grateful triumph before grabbing her parcel of cosmetics and following her guardian.

121

Lord Elliot bowed. "Victory for you. I see why my cousin finds you amusing."

Then he too was gone and Anabel sank into a chair, hoping that Lady Finch would not slander her.

She placed the picture to one side as Sally answered a knock. Anabel froze. Some part of her must have registered his step, or her senses knew his presence. She turned to meet Lord Ryder's sardonic gaze.

"Bring coffee, please," she instructed Sally.

Lord Ryder gave her a low bow. "Good day to you, Miss Harcourt."

"Not that name! I must be called Hyde."

"As you will."

"Why are you here?"

"How very unfriendly. It is the hour for making pleasant social calls."

"Bored again, my lord?"

He held a white hand to conceal a simulated yawn. "Life does grow tedious, but never with you. I find you such a comfort."

"A comfort, sir? Like a soft pillow, perhaps—or a posset administered by a nurse."

His brow crinkled. "No, I would not describe you in such terms. More like an astringent after a surfeit of oil."

"You sicken me! You have the means to make your life one of abiding interest, yet you are only a society..." She sought for a word.

"Butterfly?" supplied Lord Ryder helpfully.

His lean face expressed nothing but amusement. His hands rested lightly on a cane, his clothes were of impeccable cut and taste. He looked imperturbable.

Then she caught a flicker of vexation in his eyes. A surge of gratification intoxicated her. She held the power to annoy him when he was used only to adulation and flattery.

She turned to the table and began making her drawing materials ready for the next client.

Suddenly he was at her side. He had moved as softly as a cat and she was startled. He stared at the picture of Miss Smithson. "What a travesty of truth! Everyone knows she is not like that. I suppose you would join the conspiracy to earn another paltry florin."

Anabel set her lips and watched him pick up the portrait and hold it to the light. "Is that really how you saw her? No, it cannot be. You see with a clear sight for you gave me the truth—and my dear cousin." A smile curved his lips. "How he abhors you for it. Another diversion for which to thank you. But I cannot congratulate you on this."

Anabel drew a deep breath. "I am not here to provide you with interludes in your boring life and nothing I do is your affair."

"I choose to interest myself in you."

"What enormous conceit! You are everything I abominate!"

Beneath the shield of words her feelings were lacerated. Lord Ryder was dissolute, profligate and indolent and she longed desperately to be taken into his arms and kissed and caressed.

"I wish you to leave me alone," she lied. "Today and always, sir."

123

He said as if she had not spoken, "I take it that you have not been discovered by the Bulmores."

Anabel felt sick. "Have you heard something? Are they in town?"

"Not to my knowledge. I wondered if Elliot would inform on you."

"Why should he?"

Ryder shrugged. "He is for ever warding off his creditors. I wonder how large a reward your relatives are offering. I cannot reconcile your account of them with their eagerness to get you back."

"I daresay they wish to look well with their neighbors."

"Maybe!" He gave her a long speculative look.

She sought for a change of subject. "I was hasty just now. You will discover that I have painted Miss Smithson as I have made her look. I used my skills to change her cosmetics. This picture is quite true to life."

Ryder gave a low whistle. "Is it, by God?" He examined the drawing again. "I foresee a succession of women treading a path to your door."

He replaced the portrait and turned to her, cupping her face in his hand and gazing down at her. She should pull herself away but the moment was too exquisite a mixture of pain and pleasure. "You use your art upon your own countenance. How clever you are! And there is something about your appearance—you are not a beauty, yet..."

She struck his hand away. "I suppose it is your habit to have liberties with women without male protectors and I make a particularly splendid victim, do I not, incarcerated in these rooms by circumstances."

Clearly he resented her accusation. "I have formed no such habit. Do not forget that on one occasion I held absolute domination over you and released you."

"How very thoughtful of—"

He interrupted her savagely, "Perhaps you did not learn a lesson. You need another!"

He jerked her into his arms. Anabel stared into his eyes, feeling her senses sliding into her need. His grip tightened about her. "You are a witch. A tormenting—tantalizing—witch." He punctuated his words with soft kisses. His mouth was gentle as a whisper as he brushed her lips, eyes, lips again. It was anguish to prevent her arms from creeping round him.

At last he released her and she stood holding the edge of the table, feeling weakness steal through her as, with apparent indifference, he teased the crushed lace at his cuffs into a white froth.

"I shall be back," he said carelessly. "The game is far from over."

As his footsteps died away Anabel became rigid with self-contempt. Had she revealed her desire? Did he know she found him almost impossible to resist? She cared for him! How deeply she could not bear to examine. She would not dignify the exchange of embraces with the word love. Since her parents' death she had not known the softer emotions. Affection for the Bulmores' old nurse who had been kind to her, for the gardeners who had assisted her to cultivate herbs she needed for her experiments in paint. But love! She had been taught it had no place in marriage and Miles's wet kisses and embarrassing fumbles generated nothing but disgust. She began to long even more fervently for the day when she could declare the truth about herself and escape unwelcome attention from anybody.

Anabel's ministrations to Miss Smithson soon became the talk of the *beau monde*. Mrs. Small appeared breathless at her door to whisper, "Two ladies are on their way up. I can tell by their dress that they're rich."

Both were indeed gowned in fashionable embroidered muslin, their faces concealed by hoods drawn well forward.

Anabel waited in courteous silence until the taller woman gave a muffled exclamation and drew back her hood. It was difficult to retain a gasp of horror at a face so pitted and scarred.

The woman said, "I have not ventured outside without white paint for years. Can you help me?"

Anabel glanced at the other who shrank back. She motioned to a chair near the light. "May I know your name, ma'am? I will treat it with confidence."

"Do not tell her," hissed her companion. "If she fails, you will be a laughing stock and if she succeeds she'll make you a vulgar advertisement."

The lady in the chair shrugged. "The whole world knows my life changed when smallpox destroyed my looks. I am Mrs. Amelia Blount."

Anabel touched the ugly skin with a delicate finger. "This damage is not all from the disease."

"How perceptive of you," sneered the hooded woman.

But Mrs. Blount said kindly, "You are right, my dear. The lead paint is making havoc of my face. It is affecting my health, my physician tells me. I have dizziness and headaches and lately have been racked by internal pains. Yet I cannot go out uncovered. Will you help me as you did Miss Smithson?"

Anabel worked in silence, her deft fingers smoothing, creaming, patting, working her harmless chalk into the flesh. Here she could not depend on subtlety; the damage was too severe. When she had hidden what disfigurement she could she mixed her colors and applied them.

Her client's eyes were a pretty green which Anabel emphasized with a fine dusting of Chinese color on the lids. The mouth had mercifully escaped and she drew attention to it with rose. One fiery blemish resisted the white and this she toned down with green, to the amazement of Mrs. Blount's friend. "She will look like a clown," she protested.

Mrs. Blount stirred restlessly. "I'll not be made a laughing stock."

Anabel soothed her as she outlined her brows and lashes in deep brown before fetching a mirror.

Her client stared. "What a difference! Oh, I know that nothing can hide completely the ravages...and you say that it is all quite innocuous. I could certainly go into society like this! I look no worse—better, in fact."

The other woman snorted. "It will run when you get hot."

"Indeed, it will not," protested Anabel. "Certainly no more than any other cosmetics anyway."

Mrs. Blount smiled. "Make me a parcel of your products, my dear."

The other lady would not allow Anabel to treat her. "I shall wait and see."

Anabel could only marvel that she clung so tenaciously to a practice which she must know could actually lead to death.

Others were not so stubborn and within days Anabel's clients for beauty treatment outnumbered those wanting portraits. She made new trade cards announcing herself as "A Lady Skilled in the Art of Concealing Imperfections of the Countenance."

The cards were distributed to leading warehouses and modistes, all of whom were anxious to further Anabel's business, seeing in her success greater prosperity for theirs. For what lady, proud of her changed face, would not wish to enhance it with new clothes?

And Mr. and Mrs. Small were delighted at the exalted customers who crept through their shop and returned all smiles and benevolence, opening their purses to buy lavishly of their wares.

Eight

WHEN RYDER PAID HIS NEXT VISIT he was unable to find a vacant seat. After passing an hour leaning against a wall, arms folded, brows drawn in a frown and paying small heed to the general conversation, he begged Miss Hyde to excuse him, saying he would wait on her later.

She afforded him a cool nod and he returned after she had given up expectation of seeing him.

She continued to tidy up after her clients and greeted him calmly.

His smile was wolfish. "Are you pleased to see me or do you wish to gloat over the fact that I was wrong in supposing you unable to make a living in London?"

His infuriating habit of guessing her thoughts made her clench her teeth, but she curtseyed and asked, "Will you take wine, my lord? I regret I have little time to spare. I expect more clients."

"Your name is echoing through polite drawing rooms," said Ryder, "and having seen your handiwork I must say I think it a vast improvement on your portraits."

"How gratifying. With your approbation I shall work with increased confidence."

"One thing puzzles me," remarked Ryder.

She was jaunty. "And that is?"

"How did you obtain a license under your false name?"

She stared at him, color draining from her cheeks. At once he was at her side. "Damn my idiot tongue! Sit down! Have you any hartshorn?"

Anabel shook her head. "You devil!" she gasped. "You deliberately shocked me!"

Ryder held her pulse a fraction longer than necessary as she asked, "What license? Why should I need one?"

"All sellers of cosmetics need a license. Every item must bear an official stamp."

"And I dare not approach any official. I could be apprehended."

She considered her small capital, now almost spent on preparations from the local apothecary. She recalled the face of Mother Eve and shuddered. Only a short sojourn in the capital had made her understand how easy it was for such harridans to precipitate a country girl without advisers or money into a life of degradation.

"Why am I thwarted at every turn?" she muttered. "I have only to stay hidden for a few more weeks and I shall be safe."

She thought she detected a flicker of sympathy in Ryder's eyes before his face resumed its mocking lines. "I could lend you money," he volunteered.

"I do not need you, I am thankful to say."

He ignored the mendacious statement. "I could

keep your jewels as pledge. Or are they sold or pawned already?"

"I have had occasion before to tell you to mind your own business," she snapped, but there was no force in her rebuff. She rose and paced the room, then turned and cried, "I know what I shall do!"

A look of intense pleasure spread over the Viscount's features. "You should have entered my life years ago. What have you hatched?"

Anabel needed someone to whom to expound her plan. "I shall open a Salon. It will be a private place in which to entertain my—friends—who will, of course, be my clients. I shall not ask a fee, but shall suggest they pay me as gratitude dictates."

The Viscount's eyes narrowed in laughter. "You have an artless faith in the *ton!* How will you ascertain that you receive just dues? Many women are mean! Men too...!" he added hastily as Anabel's brows drew together.

"I may lose money sometimes," admitted Anabel, "but if they want further treatment they will have to return. I shall sell only small portions of cosmetics. I daresay most ladies will drop something into a pretty carved box which I shall purchase and leave in a spot where others can watch."

"Masterly," breathed Ryder in reverent tones.

"And I shall constantly produce new colors and treatments," continued Anabel. "I have several ideas I want to try."

He applauded. "I see I must apply to you for guidance if my speculations come to grief."

131

She was surprised. "You indulge in business ventures, my lord?"

"Nothing vulgar, I assure you, but life is dull. A man must do something besides play cards and attend racing and the like." He held up his hand at her quick intake of breath. "And I do look after my estates and people, madam! I also own ships which ply abroad and I speculate on 'Change."

"I daresay you think *me* exceedingly vulgar," flashed Anabel.

"You? Decidedly not! Headstrong—reckless—likely to tumble into dangerous situations, but vulgar? Never! With it all you manage to maintain an air of gentility."

"Well, thank you, sir. I suppose you expect me to be grateful."

"Not at all, Miss Hyde. Pray continue to follow your own bent. It is excessively interesting."

Anabel threw him a fulminating glance, then fell to musing. "My Salon must have a name. Something to do with the goddess of beauty would be appropriate. Maybe 'Temple of Venus'—no!— 'Temple of Aphrodite.' Grecian gowns are all the rage now so a Grecian goddess should be invoked..."

She paused as Lord Ryder appeared to be having difficulty with his breathing.

"You find me laughable, sir?"

"Oh, Miss Hyde...! You cannot call your Salon by such a name. Indeed, you cannot...!"

He stopped, his voice suspended, a look of unholy mirth lighting his blue eyes.

"It seems reasonable to me. What objection have you?"

Ryder spoke with deliberation. "You recall your first clients—Laughing Dorcas and Fighting Bet? I'll lay odds they came from some house labeled a temple of someone or other. If you name your Salon in such a way..."

Anabel's face flamed. She tried to speak and failed. Ryder rose and made his leisurely way toward her. For a moment she kept her gaze averted, then she turned and stared angrily into his eyes.

"You have courage," he said softly. "By God, you have." One long finger tipped her chin upwards. "And innocence—yes. It is almost inconceivable that a woman of your years, in your circumstances, could retain such innocence."

"I suppose you will waste no time in telling your friends of my mistake. It will make such a droll story."

His hand fell to his side and she was satisfied to note that she had annoyed him. "I am not a tattlemonger, madam."

"I am thankful to learn it, sir."

Further conversation was halted by the arrival of a lady escorted by her husband. Ryder bowed and left, and Anabel spent an hour working a minor miracle on a face almost ruined beyond redemption by white and red lead cosmetics. She was not especially satisfied by her efforts, but the lady and her husband were enchanted.

When asked her fee Anabel said smilingly, "Oh, there must be no talk of buying and selling here. I shall make up some packages and you shall leave whatever you consider my services worth. So much more—genteel—do not you think?"

So much more lucrative also, marveled Anabel, when she saw the gold of guineas on her table. From then on she treated her clients as visitors and they were delighted to enter the subterfuge. She purchased a pretty drum table and a carved box, and money was left in agreeable amounts.

After deliberation she called her rooms, "The Salon of Cottage Garden Beauty," a title which should appeal to the gentlefolk who followed the fashion for gardening and one which no one could fault, even Lord Ryder.

Her clientele increased and she found herself of interest to a large number of folk, some of whom came simply to watch her at work while they drank tea and gossiped. She followed Lord Ryder's advice and did not move to larger quarters, discovering that the *ton* did indeed consider a crowded Salon an enormous attraction. A need for more chairs and a good matching set of china cups sent her once more to the pawnbroker where she traded in her last asset, the diamond necklace.

Miss Smithson returned with her guardian, again accompanied by Lord Elliot. On Anabel's question the girl laughed, "Lord, no, I am having such a gay time I shall never go to Scotland."

Lady Finch gave her ward an indulgent smile, "She has several acceptable suitors now, Miss Hyde."

"And the young man in Scotland will not mind," suggested Elliot, with a sneer. "He will console himself with a lady of his own race. Men are fickle, are they not, Miss Hyde?"

Anabel sensed an antagonism which made her uneasy. She had just finished an application of cochineal Carmine and was standing back to consider the effect. She glanced at him. He was regarding her with malevolent watchfulness, clearly hoping to provoke her into dissension.

"I have little experience of the male sex, my lord," she responded and was glad when her client claimed her attention.

After Lord Elliot had left she wondered why he should make her an object of spite. She mentioned his name casually to the last client of the day.

The lady gave her a sharp look. "Have nothing to do with that one, my dear. He will promise you much and leave you ruined."

For an instant Anabel was shaken with fury at the woman's immediate assumption that she was searching for a protector. Then she calmed herself. She was forced to admit that her occupation and status were ambiguous. There would be opportunity for explanations when she attained her majority.

"I do not care for Lord Elliot," she said lightly. "I wonder only that he is so—uncharitable. He spares no one with his tongue."

The woman shrugged. "He is a jealous man. There is a great deal of wealth in the family of which he is a minor member. It is a grievance with him that his branch has small estates and income. Well, actually he has a respectable fortune, but

135

compared with the head of the family—Ryder, you know..."

She broke off to examine a pot of fragrant cream which Anabel placed by her. "What is this?"

"Lanolin and sweet marjoram, to be massaged every night into your skin, ma'am."

She cleaned the woman's face with a soft rag. "You were saying...?"

"Oh, about Elliot. Beware of him. He has a certain attraction, I suppose—wicked men are so often fascinating, are they not? But he cannot compare with Lord Ryder!"

"Is Lord Ryder wicked?"

The woman chuckled. "Wickedly attractive, I think! He has sampled everything in life, they say, and generally found it wanting. But never have I heard that he debauches innocence, and he never leaves his lights o' love in poverty. He always settles them well."

"Indeed!" Anabel's tones were frosty.

"Yes, my dear, so if you have a mind to try your luck with a protector I should make a bid for Ryder. You may succeed. He is desperate for novelty, poor man."

Anabel resisted the temptation to dab powder-filled Spanish wool on to her client's tongue. She held up a mirror and the woman studied herself. "I like it! Yes, I do like it. You were highly recommended to me and I see why. I shall return."

Anabel saw her off with relief and sank into a chair, fanning herself. What would happen when she relinquished her role as keeper of a beauty house and tried to take her rightful place in society? The world was a jungle where one could be torn apart by vicious tongues.

Sally brought her a glass of wine and a small sweet cake and she was enjoying her rest when there were footsteps on the stairs.

Anabel sighed and Sally soothed. "I daresay it is Mrs. Small."

But the noise was the clatter of fashionable heels and the high-pitched tones imperious, and Anabel waved away the tray and smoothed her hair and gown.

A moment later the door opened to the unexpected callers and Anabel felt the blood drain from her face. The younger of the two women was equally petrified by astonishment.

Anabel dragged her wits together and asked quietly, "How may I serve you, ladies?"

The older woman seated herself on a rout chair which was entirely hidden by her green striped gown. "I heard of your skill and persuaded my friend to try you. She has been plagued all her life by putrid spots which have left nasty marks. You must make her beautiful."

Anabel managed a curtsey. She needed no one to tell her that the young woman had trouble with her complexion. She knew her cousin Drusilla had spent a small fortune on remedies, without success.

She waited for Drusilla to make a comment which would destroy her anonymity. She must make plans—she must escape or in days—maybe hours—she would find herself taken back to Harcourt Manor—and Miles.

Drusilla seated herself in the chair near the window and said haughtily, "Well, woman, why do you not begin?"

Anabel's hands shook as she removed paint from Drusilla's face. She knew its spiteful lines better than her own features and it brought back memories of the years of misery. She tried to forget the past as she created a cosmetic mask to conceal the blemishes, and Drusilla admired herself with obvious surprise.

"Quite a pleasing difference," she remarked in affectedly bored tones. "How did you acquire your skill?"

"During my formative years," Anabel could not help retorting, "I was left lonely and alone and read much in a relative's book room."

A flush gave Drusilla's face a blotchy appearance and Anabel wished she had guarded her tongue.

Her cousin left a couple of florins and Sally snorted at her meanness, but Anabel said only, "I must leave here."

"Leave? But why? Everything is so nice! What will you do? Where will you go?"

"I have no idea of anything except that I must disappear."

"Madam, please...something awful could happen to you."

"Go and pack my clothes," ordered Anabel.

She had begun to drag her materials together when Drusilla walked back in. She glanced at the disordered table. "Planning to run away again?"

"Spare me your sarcasm," grated Anabel. "What

138

do you want now? I suppose you have sent word to my uncle where I am to be found."

"Well, you suppose wrong. I have come to offer help."

Anabel was baffled. She was used to a spiteful Drusilla.

Her cousin seated herself and clasped her hands. "I do not blame you for disliking Miles. I do not care for him either. I will help you stay free if you will do me a kindness."

Anabel's face was drawn as Drusilla continued, "You thought I wanted Lord Ryder because he is rich."

"It was your father's reason for getting him to the manor."

"That is true, but I like him well enough. Truly I do. I think him exciting. I would like to marry him."

Anabel's heart began to pound. "What is that to me?"

"I want you to contrive to give me an opportunity."

Anabel looked incredulously at Drusilla. Could she be so vain as to expect Ryder to want to wed her under any circumstances? He had demonstrated his contempt for her family's machinations.

"I fail to see how I can help," she stated flatly.

"Oh, of course you can. And you can also tell me what he is like—as a lover, I mean."

Anabel's eyes grew enormous. "I know nothing...!" she began.

Drusilla interrupted her, her cheeks fiery red.

"Do not play the puritan with me. Oh, how you had us fooled! Miles told us how you encouraged his advances, then turned on him like a spitfire. And when he followed you he learned from the London stage guard that you had driven off with a gentleman. Then you and Ryder posed as brother and sister at a common inn. And you pretend to be so virtuous!" jeered Drusilla.

Anabel stood clutching the back of a chair. "How dare you! How dare you assume such...such obscenities about me! I think your brother is unspeakably revolting. And as for Ryder—he helped me and gave me the best room, pretending we were related to protect my reputation."

Drusilla smiled. "You need not dissemble with me. I care nothing for your amorous adventures. Only help me ensnare Ryder and..."

"Where did you hear of the inn? Who told you?"

Drusilla opened her mouth, then closed it, peering closely at her cousin. A wary look crossed her face. "Who is best qualified to spread the information?" she asked.

"Ryder would not...!"

"Would he not?" Drusilla gave a knowing smile.

Anabel felt a hurt so great she almost cried out. She could not analyze her agony. She was incapable of calculating why the loose tongue of a man she despised should affect her so.

"I regarded him as a man of honor. At the inn he treated me as one. He behaved to me with courtesy." Except for a few moments when he kissed me and awakened my true nature! She had no idea

140

that the turbulence of her mind was revealed in her face.

Drusilla bit her lips furiously. Anabel asked, misery almost suspending her voice, "If he talks so openly might he not already have revealed my identity?"

Drusilla shrugged. "Oh, no, that would not suit my lord. I am sure he finds it more amusing to keep you here."

She could have hit upon nothing which sounded more convincing. Ryder had acknowledged to Anabel that he used her to relieve the monotony of his days.

Her wits cleared. "Wait! There was another man who saw me at the inn. A relative, Lord Elliot..."

"Oh, him!" Drusilla waved her hands dismissively. "He does not deny he saw you..."

"Deny? Is it talked about?"

"But of course! And why not? As far as anyone knows you are only a shop woman. Quite below the *ton* world. You happened to fall in with a rich lord when in desperate straits—some believe you were abandoned on the Bath road by a lover. They say that Ryder made you his mistress, then set you up here. He is known for his unusual consideration toward his abandoned female friends, and you are not so beautiful that you could hold him. Remember I learned all this when I understood you to be Miss Hyde—a stranger to me."

Anabel felt sick. She was discussed in the Salons of the *haut ton* as if she were a common courtesan. How could she ever take her place in the world?

She looked into Drusilla's merciless face. Perhaps her contempt revealed itself for Drusilla's brows drew together. "Do not presume to despise me, madam. All the years in my father's house I have had to put up with your niminy-piminy ways—your looks of dislike...."

"Your father's house! Must I remind you that Harcourt Manor is mine and that I have been treated worse than a skivvy by your family. If Papa had known that his sister would be so cruel..."

Drusilla burst out, "Why should you have so much wealth when we had none? Your papa could have left part of his fortune to us. What do you plan when you reach your majority? I suppose you will buy books, painting brushes and the like. You will travel to Florence and Rome to stare at old pictures and ruins. I know how to enjoy myself. It isn't fair!"

Anabel felt an unexpected flash of pity. "It is hard for you to be poor, Drusilla, but I would never have turned your family from the manor and I would have seen you well endowed."

Drusilla sniffed. "It's easy enough to say that now. Anyway, it is too late and it does not signify because you are going to help me marry Ryder."

"I have no power...."

"You had best think of something, for if you do not I shall inform on you. And I shall tell the authorities how you took jewels from my case while I slept. You will find yourself in Newgate and if all I've heard is true you may never emerge alive. At the best you will be returned to the manor

142

and my father will contrive that your fortune stays in the family."

Anabel compressed her shaking lips. "I have never hurt you, Drusilla."

Her cousin's harsh expression did not change. Anabel asked, "Does...does Lord Ryder know my exact state in life?"

"Certainly not! Who is there to tell him?"

That sounded logical, for Drusilla would not be in a hurry to tell the truth.

Drusilla walked to the door and turned. "I must go. My friend is waiting. I told her I lost my new lace handkerchief. All you have to do is throw me into a situation with Ryder which I can use. I will then leave you in peace."

She left and Anabel sank into a chair. Inertia stole over her. She should pack and escape, but how? According to Ryder his cousin Elliot was having her watched. And she was happy here in her work. Besides, her money was low and she must earn more. Why throw away her chances for the sake of a man who had used a guiltless situation as an amusing talking point? She would find a way of getting Drusilla and Ryder together, and she would find it excessively amusing to watch him trying to extricate himself from the grasping greed of her cousin.

She ignored the protests which rose from her innermost depths as she told Sally to unpack.

Ryder appeared in Anabel's Salon on the third day after Drusilla's visit. She was wearing a pretty gown of yellow muslin with a grass green sash and her hair, brushed into a pale gold coronet, was

143

secured with ribbons of the same green. Around her waist was a dainty frilled muslin apron which was more for ornament than use.

He seated himself and gazed about him. Anabel was engaged in work upon the face of a Duchess who had not been seen in public without white paint for ten years and was now allowing her complexion to be improved beneath the critical gaze of both women and men friends whose comments were outspoken.

The room was overflowing with the silks and scents of the *ton* world and Anabel was unaware of the fact that she glowed like a wildflower among a riot of overblown hothouse blooms. Contentment and Sally's good cooking were filling out the hollows in her face and neck. A dusting of cosmetics enhanced her appearance, and Ryder's lids narrowed as he recognized the unexpected dawning of beauty.

Although Anabel affected not to see him he was sure she was aware of his presence. When she had finished applying a coat of Talc White she allowed herself to notice him and gave a pretty start of surprise.

"How are you, my lord? I have missed you."

Anabel hoped she sounded unaffected by the heavy beating of her heart. She had received two notes from Drusilla reminding her of her demand.

Lord Ryder did not miss the calculating glances which she tried to conceal with flutters of her long dark lashes, and deliberately he rose and shook out the lace ruffles at his wrists.

"Going so soon, my lord?" asked Anabel, anxiety giving her voice a quaver.

"Stay and watch the transformation," lisped a dandy. "Truly Miss Hyde has magic in her touch, Ryder."

Anabel's client swiveled round. "Mornin', Ryder," she boomed. "'Tis true, by God! Did you ever think to see me sittin' in a chair in Bond Street bein' gone over like some damn picture?"

"If I had given the matter any thought, your Grace, I would have laid heavy odds against it," grinned Ryder.

"You'd have lost your bet then. Stay an' watch. You might not get the chance again."

Anabel's relief was so great when he reseated himself that she feared she might not have hidden it.

She began to hurry in her nervousness and was interrupted by a shriek from the Duchess. "You dug your nails in me!"

"I beg your Grace's pardon," murmured Anabel and forced herself to proceed with care.

At last the company departed, full of praise for the skill of the mistress of "The Salon of Cottage Garden Beauty" and Anabel was alone with Lord Ryder.

Nine

HIS LORDSHIP WAITED A MOMENT before saying artlessly, "Do you wish to say something particular to me, Miss Hyde?"

"I? No, sir! Whatever made you think I did?"

"Ah! Then in that case—" Ryder drew out his fob watch.

"P...pray, will you not take tea—coffee—with me," gasped Anabel. She felt hot. What a sorry mess she was making of this.

Ryder made it easier for her by accepting a cup of coffee and even eating a small cheesecake, pointing out in bland accents that although he did not normally eat between breakfast and dinner, today was an exception.

Anabel rose instantly to his bait. "Why so, sir?"

"Why, because you asked me, ma'am."

"Would...would you then do anything I asked?"

Ryder's brows rose and Anabel felt a tide of pink wash over her.

"Try me," he invited.

Anabel gulped. It went against all her inclination but she forced the words through her lips. "I...I have a desire to see the *haut ton* at play. I hear much talk of splendid occasions."

"My dear Miss Hyde! Where would you care to go?"

Anabel was taken aback. She had half expected him to be shocked—or even angry. He knew she was of good birth, but according to Drusilla she was set apart from polite society by the rumor of her promiscuity. And Ryder was the man who had betrayed her.

She stared at him, her tongue trembling with reproaches and insults.

He smiled benignly. "If you had not spoken in honeyed accents I would swear you are vexed with me."

"Oh, no, sir, I am not," lied Anabel. "What could you have done to make me vexed?"

She waited breathlessly as Ryder flicked a speck of dust from his sleeve. He looked up. "Nothing, ma'am; how may I serve you?"

"I wish to go to Vauxhall Gardens, sir."

"Really! And what part do I play in your proposed expedition?"

Anabel lowered her lids. "I thought you could escort me."

There was a short silence during which Ryder tapped his fingers softly on the arm of his chair. "I am flattered. If you wish to join a party to Vauxhall I do not understand why you require my presence."

"Not a party, sir. I thought just you and I..."

This time the silence seemed to last an eternity before Lord Ryder said, "This is a most unexpected request, ma'am. Some men might consider it an invitation."

"To what, sir?" she snapped, losing her purpose momentarily in fury.

Something flickered in the blue eyes calmly regarding her. "If you want favors you must learn to behave more prettily, madam. I take it that it is not my person with which you are smitten. You see me merely as a suitable companion for an evening stroll."

"That is it exactly! I will wear a mask and no one will know you are with a woman not considered your own level. I would be so diverted by..."

"Spare me." His lordship concealed a yawn and Anabel's eyes crackled with sparks.

He smiled as he got lazily to his feet. "Shall I call for you tonight?"

"Tonight?"

"Why not? The evening promises to be fine. Would you prefer to postpone our engagement?"

"No, sir, but..."

"I am seldom free, Miss Hyde. I was to visit a friend this evening, but he is indisposed."

"Oh, very well! Let it be tonight."

"You are an enigma," commented Ryder. "One moment all soft smiles and charm; the next claws and sharp tongue. Well, at least you are different from the general run of female."

Anabel kept her clenched fists hidden in the folds of her gown. "Will we be able to eat supper in one of the boxes, my lord? I have heard they are a feature of Vauxhall."

"You are correct, though not all supper parties are as intimate as ours promises to be. Supper it shall be. I will order it."

He promised to return at eight o'clock and left. Anabel leaned on the wall, her knees almost unable to support her. Then she wrote a letter which Sally delivered to Drusilla. A reply arrived and she and Sally set to work stitching a suitable garment for the evening.

As the London clocks chimed the hour the Viscount presented himself and Anabel's already unsteady heart gave a lurch. He looked devastatingly attractive in cream pantaloons and black, buckled shoes; a black cutaway coat revealed a deep red silk waistcoat whose color was repeated in the ruby set in the gold of his single ring. A slender gold chain held a fob watch and his hair was dressed without powder.

When he saw Anabel he frowned. "You did not say you would be masquerading in fancy clothes. I expected to find you looking delightful in one of your new gowns."

"Your own appearance makes up for any lack of distinction in mine, sir," murmured Anabel.

The compliment was from her heart, but her agitation gave her voice a sarcastic quality which Ryder did not miss.

His blue eyes traveled the full length of her black domino with its concealing hood and his hand went up to touch the black velvet mask.

Anabel stammered, "I...I gave the matter of our outing much thought. I concluded that it would not do for you to be seen with a...beauty-shop keeper."

His eyes seemed to pierce her skull. "How incredibly considerate of you, Miss Hyde."

"There is also the matter of my security. I do not know if my relatives are in town. I must not be seen by them."

Ryder shrugged. "I am convinced you must go out in heavy disguise." He paused. "May I suggest that we go to Ranelagh instead. It is far more suited to a lady's entertainment. Many cits attend Vauxhall and one can find oneself in proximity with any number of working folk."

"Of which I am one," reminded Anabel. "I wonder you dare to be seen with me at all."

Ryder gave her a long look. "Ah, but you have made it certain that I shall not be embarrassed by accompanying a lady from so humble a sphere."

Anabel had asked for the snub and could only repeat with finality, "I wish to go to Vauxhall."

He held out his arm and she placed her gloved hand upon it, then he led her to his elegant town carriage and they were driven through cobbled streets, across the crowded bridge over the River Thames, to the gates of Vauxhall Gardens.

Anabel forgot her agitation as they wandered together along the tree-lined avenues where hundreds of colored lanterns gave the leaves an exotic glow and threw patches of multicolored lights on the grass. She took a deep breath. "I had not realized I missed the sweetness of the country air. What a splendid place this is. I could almost imagine myself back home. I used often to take long walks alone."

"Well, it would not do for you to walk alone here!"

Anabel said impulsively, "Oh, I did not mean

151

that I did not want you here. It is most kind of you to escort me."

She was reminded suddenly of the purpose of her visit and her exaltation died. Her voice was flat as she asked the time.

"It does not signify," replied Ryder. "Would you care to see the Music Room?"

Anabel hesitated and Ryder sighed and looked at his watch. "It is nine o'clock. Early evening in fact, though I must remember you are a working lady. At what hour do your clients impose themselves upon you?"

"I do not consider them an imposition!" she declared. "Without them I could not stay in London."

"You have just said you prefer the country," pointed out Ryder.

Anabel felt like stamping her black half boot in rage. "You always find something to argue about."

"You react so gratifyingly quickly." The Viscount's tones were bland, but there was a deep meaning in his voice which gave her a flutter of alarm.

"Let us go to the Music Room, sir."

"There is no hurry."

He slid his arm about her waist and drew her to his side as they passed a couple in an equally close embrace. She was torn between an impulse to jerk herself away and a desire to press her body closer to the muscular one beside her.

Remembering her purpose she allowed her hand to creep up and cover the one clasped beneath her breast. She heard the Viscount sigh softly, and as they reached an alcove half-hidden by bushes he drew her into the shadows.

Slowly he turned her toward him. His lips explored her face. He drew off her mask and slid his mouth over her eyes, following the contour of her smooth, scented cheek to her waiting lips.

"God, Anabel, you are a surprising creature," he murmured. "One moment all icy dignity, the next a yielding morsel to set a man's senses aflame."

Anabel gave a small, dry sob and Ryder drew his head back and touched her mouth with a gentle finger. "What is it, my dear? I could swear you find my lovemaking welcome, yet always there is an element of sadness—almost of despair. Cannot you let go your reserve? I will not harm you."

"You trifle with me—as you have with many women." Her voice was almost soundless.

"That is not so. I find you far more diverting than any woman I have known."

"Diverting!" Furious, she thrust herself from his embrace. "That is *all* I am! An amusement! Someone to help you pass an hour or two of your boring existence."

Ryder laughed and she shivered. "My dear Miss Hyde, you were the one who suggested that we come to Vauxhall alone. You refused my suggestion that we make up a party. Just what am I supposed to infer?"

Anabel walked quickly from the alcove and he joined her on the walk. She felt only a desire to end this farce as soon as possible.

"Where do they serve supper?" she demanded,

replacing her mask and failing to tie the strings with unsteady fingers.

"Pray allow me," said Ryder and drew the strings together, securing them with a bow. He then pulled the hood over her head, murmuring, "Such a pity to hide your pretty hair."

She felt even more nervous at his compliments and asked again to be conducted to supper.

"Are you famished, Miss Hyde? From the looks of you when we met I took you to be someone who cared little for the pleasures of the table."

"I cannot eat when I am worried or unhappy."

"Pitiful little poor relation," mocked the Viscount gently. "Kept in the background and ill used. Was there no one who cared?"

"Once. There was a nursemaid and they dismissed her."

"Because she grew fond of you?"

Anabel fell silent. She had been ten years old when the elderly Bulmore nurse died and her place was taken by a good-hearted woman. Anabel had warmed to affection for which she was starved, and the nurse was amazed to discover that the child knew nothing of her true circumstances. In an effort to help her look to the future she told her that she was true mistress of Harcourt Manor and heiress to a substantial fortune. Money meant little to Anabel, but when she reached her eleventh birthday she asked her uncle if she might use some of her wealth to buy a puppy. His rage terrified her and the nurse was sent away without a reference.

Anabel waited a further year before braving her

uncle's wrath a second time to ask in what circumstances her inheritance was to be given her.

"Under any circumstances I choose," was his reply.

When her cousin, Miles, pursued her with his vile embraces it had been he, in red and sweating rage, the marks of her slap prominent on his face, who had blurted out the truth. "Skinny, ugly bitch! You had best get to like me because Papa says we are to be married. I am to be the sacrifice to get your fortune!"

Anabel had gathered courage to creep to the study at night where she found a copy of her father's will, bequeathing everything to her, either on marriage or on attaining her majority at the age of one and twenty. No conditions were attached.

Memories filled Anabel's eyes with tears which she dashed away.

Ryder said with concern, "Your musings seem painful to you."

"It is all past. My nurse was dismissed for talking too much. I do not wish to discuss it."

But I will always remember, she thought. Money attracts husbands however plain and boring a woman might be. She would never know if she was truly desired. Miles Bulmore had taught her that.

They were walking again beneath the lighted trees and Anabel tried to hurry, but his lordship held her back firmly.

"Where is this supper room?" she demanded.

"Tables are laid in alcoves in the Chinese Pavilion," answered Ryder. "You have no need to be reticent with me. I would never betray you, Miss Hyde."

Heat seared Anabel's body as she felt the shame of her intention. She faltered, then hastened on, telling herself that the only way to placate Drusilla was to obey her. Perhaps Ryder would understand. He could deal with her cousin, she assured herself.

Seated at a table Ryder suggested that she remove her mask. Anabel shook her head and he lifted a shoulder. "Very well. I ordered supper. I trust you approve of my choice. Please do not hesitate to say if you do not."

Anabel scarcely heard him. It was after nine and soon she must begin the charade.

Lord Ryder clicked his fingers and a waiter appeared. He knew the Viscount and showed no surprise at the sight of a masked lady alone with him. He probably brings many women here, she fumed, and used the idea to soothe her gnawing conscience.

"I am glad you feel hungry," remarked Ryder. "I have called for poached salmon with horse radish and preserved peaches in cream. Will that do?"

"Yes, oh, yes, my lord," muttered Anabel.

"A somewhat disappointing response. I took trouble to tempt your appetite."

"I have never been choosy over food."

"Perhaps you were denied the opportunity. I have always paid proper attention to my well-being."

The waiter materialized with wine. Anabel

shook her head, then nodded at the bottle, feeling she could not endure another altercation, however slight.

She sipped at the pale wine and the glow gave her courage. She could not do justice to the meal, but managed a little of each dish.

Lord Ryder sounded more solicitous than ever. "Are you not happy to take supper with me? I remember that you said you could never eat when unhappy or worried. Can I not assume you to be content now?"

Anabel choked a little on a piece of peach. She looked at him and realized he was watching her closely, his eyes alight with laughter. For once he was not mocking her and she responded, her hand going out in an involuntary gesture. He took her fingers and kissed them gently.

"Please take off your mask, my dear," he begged.

A distant clock struck ten and the moment was destroyed. She was conscious of an inward warning that she might be about to spoil more than the passing evening, but she must go on. She must never forget that Lord Ryder was notorious for light dalliance. He must not cloud her first aim which was to stay away from Miles Bulmore and his parents.

She managed to give a convincing cry of alarm as she clutched her neck. "I have lost my necklace!"

The Viscount looked suitably perturbed. "Not your diamonds!"

"What?" Anabel had forgotten that he had seen

her jewels. "No, a necklace of coral. I treasure it. My lord, would you be so kind as to see if I have dropped it somewhere along the walk. I know I had it on when we arrived."

The waiter intervened. "I will search, madam."

"No!" Anabel could not keep panic from her voice and was not surprised to see Ryder's eyes narrow. Then he rose, dismissed the waiter, and bowed.

"I will look for the necklace," he agreed pleasantly, and Anabel watched his lithe figure as it vanished from sight among the trees.

At once a figure darted from the next alcove. The woman dressed exactly the same as Anabel hissed, "Come on! Will you sit there all night?"

Anabel allowed Drusilla to take her place. "I cannot imagine what you think to achieve," she said. "As soon as you speak he'll know it is not me."

"I will deal with the problem, I promise you. I was in tucks to see you hold his hand. And what were you doing in the bushes? I did not know you had so much coquetry in you!"

"I was not...!"

"Oh, go, for heaven's sake! If he returns now it will all have been for nothing."

Anabel ran blindly into the shadows and reached a wide path where she raced beneath a series of classical arches, darting round astonished couples, evading the clutches of drunken young men out for sport.

She had believed herself to be heading for the

gate to the road and drew up in panic as she realized that before her lay the broad river Thames.

A party of revelers was just stepping on shore from one of the boats and pulling her purse from her pocket she took a step toward it. Then she was grabbed from behind.

"Let me go," she implored. "Oh, please let me go!"

A voice she knew filled her with horror. Lord Elliot held her arms bruisingly tight as he gasped, "Damn you! It is years since I ran! I might have died of an apoplexy...."

"What do you want? Let me go, my lord!"

"If you think we have gone to such trouble to allow you to disappear from the scene you are much mistaken. The farce must be played in full."

He slipped his arm about her waist and held her close as he dabbed at his sweating face with a handkerchief. In his green brocade and satin coat, orange striped waistcoat and black pantaloons, his face hectic with paint and exertion, his eyes glittering with evil, he could have passed for a devil.

Anabel felt cold. "What do you mean? I came here on a task known only to—a certain lady," she stammered.

She was not surprised when he answered, "Your cousin, Drusilla. And a cunning game she is playing. Now you will accompany me back to the others and we shall proceed."

Another man arrived and between them they hurried her back to where a party of several men and women waited. They had been drinking heav-

159

ily and were anticipating a fine joke. Anabel's domino and mask were torn from her and hurled into the bushes and a blue silk cloak pulled onto her shoulders.

"Pray she may have kept him interested without speaking," muttered Elliot as Anabel was propelled to the Chinese Pavilion.

In the supper alcove Anabel saw Drusilla. She had moved to seat herself next to Ryder and her arm was about his neck. Her lips were on his and his arm lay round her waist.

Anabel strove to pull herself free. She felt sick anger, loathing of Drusilla and her wicked lies and scheming. She also knew she was burning with jealousy, but had no time to come to terms with it before the couple in the booth looked round at her companions' noisy explosion of mirth.

Lord Elliot stepped forward, "Good evening, cousin. How delightful to meet you here on such a fine night. Will you not introduce us to your lady?"

Ryder's gaze flickered over Anabel briefly before he removed the black mask from Drusilla's face.

"I think you need no introduction," he said evenly. "I am sure that Miss Bulmore is known to you all."

"You sly dog!" lisped a painted beau, gesturing toward the couple with a long beribboned cane. "I had no notion that you and Miss Bulmore were so close."

The others chorused agreement.

"When is the announcement to be made?" asked Elliot.

Ryder rose and shook out the ruffles at his wrists. "What announcement?"

"Of your betrothal! What else!" demanded a buxom woman. "A gentleman would never bring a lady out in so private a manner if they were not promised to one another."

Ryder's glance traveled slowly over the woman. "Would he not?" was all he said, but the company fell silent.

Drusilla sprang to her feet. "No, he would not," she cried. "Can you deny that we walked in the gardens? That we paused in the shade of the trees? That we have been alone for at least two hours? That you have just plighted yourself to me in a kiss?"

"I agree that there are plenty of witnesses to say I kissed you, Miss Bulmore. I have kissed many women, but have not considered marrying them any more than I consider making you my wife. We all know that an attempt at subterfuge was made. You failed completely. To pull off such a trick you need a young pigeon with his down wet from the egg. I have not been deceived for a single moment."

He stepped forward to confront Anabel. His tone was low but clear to all. "Did you think I would mistake your cousin for you? I am not so foolish! I have been curious to know how your melodrama would proceed. Perhaps I *was* deceived—a little— I almost thought—but no matter. I shall not make the same error again."

She tried to speak but her tongue clove to the roof of her mouth. His finger went up and flicked her cheek lightly. "I had not realized you bore me such a grudge, madam."

He left, and the voices round Anabel blurred as she felt her senses swimming in the maze of her anger toward Drusilla and her misery at Ryder's scalding contempt.

Ten

LOUD WERE THE PROTESTATIONS of indignation on Drusilla's behalf, but nothing could disguise the fact that the company found her discomfiture exceedingly comic.

In the end Drusilla begged for relief from advice which ranged from suggestions that she should conceal herself abroad to persuasion to apply to the courts with an action for damage to her sensibilities.

They had arrived at the gates and Anabel, finding herself forgotten, managed to secure a hackney to take her home.

She slept little that night, her mind disturbed by the ever-recurring memory of the look in Ryder's eyes before he left her.

In the morning, pale, and suffering from a headache, she felt ill equipped to endure the eruption of Drusilla into her rooms.

She gave her opinion of Anabel and her mode of living, Ryder's character and reputation, before raving, "I suppose you think it as amusing as the others! What a story to circulate the London drawing rooms." She wrung her hands. "I *will* think of a way to escape ridicule. We could deny the whole thing. No, that will not serve."

She stared suddenly at Anabel. "I have it!" Her small eyes shone with relief. "A capital notion! I fear it will put you in an unfavorable light, but I shall confuse the gossips so no one will really know the truth."

Anabel's questions were disregarded as Drusilla hurried to the door, pausing to call back that she would be back quite soon for more cosmetics.

Anabel continued to work that day, smiling at witticisms, instructing Sally to serve refreshments, covering her deep hurt.

She had no time to analyze her suffering. All that had happened, she rationalized, was that a few worthless members of the *ton* had played a prank on a victim well able to care for himself.

She owed Ryder nothing. He looked upon her as an amusement when he had nothing better with which to interest himself.

She was attending her last client of the day when the man who filled her mind strolled in and seated himself, lounging back in a nonchalant way. One glance showed Anabel that his smile did not reach his eyes.

She dreaded a confrontation and prolonged the beauty treatment until the lady complained that she would miss her first engagement.

Then Anabel and the Viscount were alone. He continued to relax as she began to clear away her pots and pestles. The silence became unbearable. She glanced his way to see him delicately taking snuff.

The action seemed unendurably provocative and she flashed, "If you are come to make reproaches, then get them over and done with."

"Reproaches? I am here to listen to your explanation of last night's excellent performance."

She faced him, her hands gripping the table behind her. "You made it clear to me that you had already made your assessment of my actions."

"What did you expect? A congratulatory bouquet?"

Anabel flushed. "I . . . I did not know that Drusilla . . . that is to say..."

"Are you about to tell me that the stupid scheme to trap me into a public declaration was entirely unknown to you?"

"Of course not! I knew that Drusilla was plotting to—attract you. She told me what to wear and suggested I ask you to take me to Vauxhall. I had no idea that others would be involved. I did not realize she could be so brazen. It was a terrible shock...."

Anabel looked down at her feet, tears stinging the backs of her eyes. Then the Viscount was in front of her, loosening the grip of her fingers on the table, holding her hands in his.

"I believe you," he said. "Look at me."

She raised her head and stared into his eyes.

He shook his head. "What is it about you? If any other woman had treated me with half the provocation I would teach her a lesson she would not easily forget. Yet—once more—I feel only... kindness toward you."

Kindness! Anabel felt a surge of disappointment

165

and her eyes darkened. The Viscount's gentleness vanished and he laughed sardonically. When she tried to move her hands he gripped them harder, then lifted them and with deliberation kissed each finger and her palms. She could not free herself unless she wished to partake in a degrading struggle and she suffered his caresses, denying her secret awareness that every touch of his mouth on her was bringing back the yearning he provoked.

Still holding her hands Ryder said softly, "I sense a creature of fire in you, Anabel."

"I did not say you could use my name," she gasped.

"Yes, a creature of fire. One who will give herself to one man only, and when she does, I think that man will be exceedingly blessed."

Abruptly he released her and she sank onto a chair, her knees feeling liquid.

"Why did you obey Drusilla, Anabel?"

She sighed. "She threatened to tell Miles where I am."

"So that was it. When I had time to think I knew there must be a rational explanation for your conduct. It puzzles me why your relatives are so desperately anxious to have you back."

At her slight gesture of protest he grinned, "Oh, *I* know your worth, but from what you said it is clear that they do not. So why should a poor, downtrodden female relative inspire such malignant determination to keep you in their home? And what possesses them to want you to marry Miles Bulmore?"

Anabel could think of no reply. Ryder was getting dangerously close to questions she would not answer. For the first time in her life she was making a friend. She needed him. It seemed they could laugh and talk together; they could even quarrel and remain on good terms. And all this had been achieved when he believed her to be destitute and existing by use of her wits. Her friendship with him was a precious jewel which must not be altered.

"Do my questions rate such deep consideration?" asked Ryder. "Can it possibly be that you have a *tendre* for Miles?"

"I find him repugnant! But...but he thinks he is in love with me and his parents deny him nothing."

The lie hung on the air between them.

"I see," said Ryder. He bowed and left.

Anabel paced the floor. Would he return this time? He had looked angry—disappointed. She hugged her arms about her body, remembering the feel of his. His kisses were growing more tender. She thrust the thought from her. He had the pick of society's loveliest women—he would never turn to her. The sooner he grew tired of his casual embraces the sooner they could establish their friendship. And the sooner she would regain control over the wanton imaginings which tormented her.

The following day brought an invitation from Ryder. "Dear Miss Hyde," it read, "since you are prepared to go out masked I would be honored if you would accompany me to a Masquerade at the residence of her Grace the Duchess of Stowebridge.

I will send my carriage for you at eight o'clock two nights from now."

The impudence of the man! Anabel crumpled the letter and threw it in the direction of the fire. Then she retrieved it and smoothed it and read it again. Damn Lord Ryder! Did he think he could command her? Was he so sure she would go with him? For, of course, she had every intention of doing so.

Sally was excited at the idea. "The Duchess of Stowebridge! What will you say? How will you talk to her?"

Anabel laughed. "You need not ask, for you have served her with coffee when she came here."

Sally's mouth dropped open. "That Duchess! The one who came for a beauty treatment? I never thought of her as being grand. She acted quite ordinary." She blushed at her presumption.

Anabel was glad they had just completed a gown of pale orange crepe trimmed with lace. Again she and Sally fashioned a domino, this time in satin the color of the gold flecks in her eyes, and silver ribbons to catch the glints in her hair. Her mask was of the mandatory black velvet and before putting it on she surveyed herself in the glass on the night of the Masquerade and thought, for the first time, that some might find her desirable.

She was called for by a liveried footman who conducted her to a crested carriage where she was surprised to find a lady who introduced herself as Mrs. Jane Marriot, a relative of Ryder's.

She chatted volubly all the way to Grosvenor Square and Anabel learned that she was the widow of a clergyman and had been gratified to receive a summons to chaperon a young lady to a ball.

In the large tiled hall in the house in Grosvenor Square Mrs. Marriot greeted old school friends and Ryder appeared to escort the ladies. He looked overpoweringly attractive in his dark, elegantly tailored coat, worn with white buckskin breeches and silk stockings. The buckles on his black shoes were scattered with tiny diamonds and his cravat was secured with a gold pin set with a single diamond. His eyes appraised her through the slits of his mask. She placed a gloved hand on his arm and they began to ascend the stairs.

"How did you know me?" asked Anabel.

"I never imagined I would find it difficult," he replied blandly, "but I insured success by engaging Mrs. Marriot to chaperon you. I knew I would be able to pick you out anywhere by her ceaseless talk."

Mrs. Marriot was behind them, still talking volubly, and Anabel suppressed an unladylike giggle. She looked about her surreptitiously and was relieved to see that although most ladies were gowned in splendor and wearing superb jewels, she would be able to hold her place without worry. She wondered where Sally had gained such skills in making gowns and dressing hair.

They arrived at the head of the stairs and the Duchess tapped Ryder with her ivory fan. "You cannot hide behind a mask from me, sir. Do not forget I dandled you on my knee when you were in long skirts."

"I would never try to deceive you, your Grace," replied Ryder, a laugh in his voice.

The Duchess frowned a little. "There is nothing you would not dare. That has been your trouble."

Her heavy gold skirts swung as she turned to Anabel. "Good evening, Miss Hyde. Ryder said he would bring you."

Anabel went cold. Surely the Duchess would not take exception publicly to her presence. She knew her only as the proprietress of a beauty salon. Anabel felt Ryder stiffen as the same thought occurred to him and she knew, with surprising instinct, that he would defend her.

But her Grace only smiled, revealing a couple of gaps in her teeth which she hid at once with an expert unfurling of her fan.

"You need not flash your eyes at me, Ryder. Perhaps Miss Hyde can succeed in taming you where others have failed."

Anabel was warm with embarrassment, but Ryder took the Duchess's heavily ringed hand in his and kissed it.

They moved to make way for the next group and walked into the ballroom which was hot from the immense throng and the hundreds of wax candles. Anabel was fascinated. Assemblies such as this should have been her right for at least four years past. She should be able to greet members of the *haut ton* with friendship. She knew that many of the shrilled words of affection, as disguises were penetrated, were all part of society sham, yet she was shaken with rage at her relatives who had prevented her entry into her world.

170

Perhaps now she never would be part of it, for even when she reached her majority she might be rejected as a woman who had engaged in trade.

Ryder bent close to her ear. "Can you share your musings? They seem melancholy."

Anabel fluttered her fan in excellent imitation of the Duchess. "La, no, sir, you are mistóok! I am all happiness at being here."

His lordship looked down his aristocratic nose at her. "Spare me the affectation! I can obtain all I need of that from other women."

Other women! How quick he was to make her aware that she was one among many to share his favor.

He took her gently, but firmly, by the elbow and steered her to the supper room where he ordered iced champagne. "I spoke thoughtlessly," he admitted. "You resemble no one I ever met. That is why I find you so...interesting."

Anabel tried to be glad that she provided him with interest as she sipped her wine and listened to his murmured comments, some scurrilous, but always amusing, about those whom he recognized.

Her mood lightened. When they heard music his lordship took her back to the ballroom. Rows of mirrors heightened the effect of light and reflected with dazzling brilliance the colors of the clothes and the myriad multihued sparkle of gems. Anabel drew a deep breath of pleasure as the orchestra began to play again. Ryder held out his arm and she took a step back.

"You...you are asking me to dance?"

His brows climbed. "You sound surprised! It is customary for a gentleman to dance with his lady."

"I am not your lady, sir."

Her tones were low, but one or two people who had taken their places for the minuet glanced their way and the lines that scored either side of the Viscount's mouth deepened.

"You are my guest and I expect you to dance with me."

Anabel's face flamed. "Please..." she begged, in an insistent whisper. "I . . . I cannot . . ."

Ryder took her arm and attempted to propel her toward the lines of dancers already beginning their obeisance, but she hung back with equal determination until he glared in angry bafflement. She took advantage of a momentary release of his grip to escape curious eyes and hurry through the first door she came to. She found herself in an antechamber with no other outlet, and before she could retrace her steps Lord Ryder appeared outlined against the brightness of the ballroom, before he half closed the door behind him. There was a single branch of candles burning over the fire grate and Anabel could not see the expression in his eyes, but his voice told her of his extreme displeasure.

"Have I deserved such treatment from you, madam?"

"You should not take things for granted," she said flatly.

"I asked you to a masked ball...."

"You commanded me, sir."

"I find it difficult to believe that you were afraid to refuse."

"Really! I suppose you might find it even more difficult to understand that a man who uses a woman as entertainment may be used by her in her turn."

"Is that why you came?"

Anabel was silent, but words seethed in her brain. It was true she had longed for a glimpse of the *ton* world, but she would never have entrusted herself to a man for an introduction unless she had faith in his honor. No, face up to the truth, she admonished herself. You wanted to go with him. You always want to be with him even though you know his reputation as a rakehell.

"I asked you a question, madam!"

The Viscount's voice was icy now and Anabel said, "I expected only to watch a little lively entertainment."

"Nonsense! You must have expected to dance. Or if you did not feel inclined, you should have told me earlier—and not have allowed me to act a fool in public."

"Is that what distresses you? Shall I return and make a public announcement of apology to you?"

Ryder strode to her and caught her arms in cruel hands.

"Let me go, sir! You are hurting me!"

"I thought you possessed a nobler spirit. I felt, for the only time in my life, that I had discovered a woman who...well, no matter." He released her. "I will take you home."

Anabel passed with him head held high to stop

with a gasp as a dark figure moved. Someone had entered during their quarrel and stood hidden in the gloom behind the door.

"Who the hell are you?" demanded Ryder.

"Hoity-toity!"

Anabel swallowed hard as she recognized the Duchess's voice, then she curtseyed.

"I saw the pretty scene in the ballroom," remarked her Grace, seating herself on a bench and spreading her skirts about her. "I decided to follow. What a mishmash, Ryder. How can you behave so stupidly?"

Lord Ryder's voice was cool, but Anabel felt an insane desire to giggle at the way the Duchess reduced him to the naughty boy she remembered. "Permit us to depart, madam. I wish to return Miss Hyde to her home. It seems I was mistaken when I thought she would enjoy a dance with me."

The Duchess stamped one of her well-shod feet. "Have you no wits? She is a poor girl forced to earn her living, though 'tis easy for anyone in their senses to see she has more breedin' than many a court lady. But one thing she don't know is how to dance a minuet. Am I right, my girl?"

Anabel nodded, her silvery hair catching the candle gleams. "Yes, your Grace."

Ryder struck his thigh with an angry fist. "Why did you not say so? Oh! I did not give you opportunity, did I? I tried to drag you into a dance..."

"Oh, not drag, my lord," protested Anabel, a catch in her voice.

"I insisted most firmly, then."

"Will you have done?" demanded the Duchess.

"Talk—talk—talk! The music can be heard clearly from here. It is a *danse à deux*, Miss Hyde. Show her the steps, Ryder, and I will play chaperon since I prevented your agitated hen, Mrs. Marriot, from following you."

Ryder and Anabel stared at one another, then his lordship smiled. "Will you honor me with your company in a minuet, madam?"

Anabel murmured an assent and Ryder said, "There are only four main figures. All steps for both lady and gentleman begin on the right foot. You need to remember the demi-coupe and a fleuret done to six counts. So!"

He demonstrated with athletic grace before taking her hand and leading her into the dance. They moved with the stately precision demanded by the dance's refined pattern of manners and Anabel picked up the steps quickly. She became absorbed in the rhythm, moving slowly in time with her partner, taking first his right hand, then his left, and by the time he led her round with both hands and the music stopped, she was tingling with pleasure.

She had forgotten the Duchess and was surprised at the sound of applause. "Excellently done, my dear. Now there is nothing to prevent you taking your place in the remainder of the opening minuets. Can you perform any country dances?"

"Yes, your Grace. One or two, anyway. I had a kind nursery maid who taught me."

In her high spirits Anabel did not notice the keen look the Duchess shot her at this mention of a nursery maid. The next two hours were a source of immense pleasure as she and Ryder took the floor for almost every dance.

At first she protested, "You should partner other ladies, sir."

Ryder smiled down at her. "Not at all, Anabel. It is customary to pick up a fan from the table and remain its owner's partner for the evening."

"I did not lay down a fan...."

"Did you think I would allow some other man to monopolize your charming company?"

They supped off poached salmon, chicken mousse and buttered oranges, and Anabel felt her senses becoming turbulent with the joy she experienced in Ryder's company.

As the evening progressed it became evident that many men drank as deeply as her uncle and his cronies, and as they returned to the ballroom after supper, a clumsy sot stumbled against her, tearing the delicate lace at her breast as he sought to steady himself.

Ryder's face darkened in rage, but the man's mumbled apologies were genuine, if blurred by drink. Anabel sped to the room set aside for ladies, where maids waited with needles and thread for just such an emergency.

As she settled behind a silk-lined screen while she waited, she began to realize how tired she felt. She had to rise early, unlike the rest of the guests, many of whom had not seen the morning sun for years.

She had fallen into a half-doze when voices from the other side of the screen roused her.

"They say he met her on the road. Do you recall the storm when so many travelers were stranded? She looked like a bedraggled hen, I daresay."

A second woman shrilled her laughter. "What a joke! What happened then?"

"He took her to an inn. Some say they had separate rooms, but everyone knows *he* would not let such an opportunity slip by. I warrant one of the beds was never used."

"How droll! And now she is set up as a beauty counselor. I wonder what other services she offers her protector!"

There was a burst of laughter. "Is she here tonight?"

"Who can tell? Who knows what lies behind the masks?"

"How vastly diverting!"

"That is not all! Apparently she persuaded Drusilla Bulmore to play a fine game. She got her to leave Ryder in a booth in Vauxhall while the cunning beauty adviser slipped into Miss Bulmore's place in disguise and attempted to compromise him."

"No! Did she really suppose she would trap him? She knows little of our noble Viscount if she thinks to intimidate him."

They left, their sibilant voices beginning on another reputation, and Anabel sat feeling sick. The maid had to speak twice.

"Your gown is ready, ma'am. You may return to the ballroom."

Anabel's tears blurred her vision. She could not

imagine how such gossip was being spread, though the story about Vauxhall was being told by Drusilla with one vital change. She had reversed their roles and Anabel was being castigated as a schemer without principles. Worse! She was condemned as little better than a whore! Drusilla's companions at Vauxhall would not care what story gained credence so long as their evil mischief-making gave them amusement. And as for Lord Elliot, he would be prepared to connive in anything which annoyed Lord Ryder.

She would not remain here for further humiliation. She would leave at once, alone, and escape the bitter tongues.

As she handed the maid a vail and left the room the clocks began to chime midnight. She looked quickly along the corridors, deserted save for servants, and hurried in the direction of the front door. A hand grasped her arm none too gently and Ryder rasped, "The way to me lies in the opposite direction. Running away? The unmasking is about to begin."

Anabel stared into his merciless eyes. Had he brought her here to watch her final debasement? Was he in league with her other tormentors? In her exhausted misery she could not think coherently and she would not demean herself by feeble struggling beneath the interested looks of footmen who hurried past with trays.

She was hustled back to the ballroom as the chimes died away and the Duchess mounted the orchestra podium. The company fell silent. "My lords, ladies, gentlemen, let the unmasking commence."

The screams of mirth, the cries of mock amazement, the confirmations sounded to Anabel like barnyard noises. She saw Drusilla and her escort unmask and realized that her cousin was with Lord Elliot. Many of her clients were there and Anabel shrank from the idea of the essays of barbed wit, the sneers which would wing her way. She tried to slip away, but once again was prevented by Ryder, who stood, the strings of his mask curled over his fingers, his face expectant.

She remained the only person still masked and cries and taunts filled the air. One bold fop half raised his hand to tear at her mask, but was repelled by the expression in Ryder's eyes.

Anabel slowly lifted her hands when an imperious voice commanded, "No, my dear! Leave it where it is!"

The Duchess walked to her side and faced the company. "She shall remain as she wishes."

Protests echoed to the domed ceiling and the Duchess smiled. "I form the rules in my house."

She turned to Anabel. *"La belle masquée* shall please herself."

She gestured to the musicians who struck up for a cotillion, a dance which Anabel did not know. She sank onto a rout chair and Drusilla and Elliot joined her.

"Well, that got you out of trouble nicely, did it not?" jeered Drusilla. "You needn't think to get away with it. I know who you are."

"And I daresay you will lose no time in betraying her," said Lord Ryder.

Elliot wafted a fan before his heavily rouged face. "Why not? One rule for all!"

"Why?" demanded Ryder.

"Why...why because it has always been so. At a masked ball one unmasks at midnight."

"The lady has changed the pattern," grated Ryder. He bowed to Anabel. "Allow me to take you for refreshment, ma'am."

His glance at Elliot was one of such contemptuous dismissal that Elliot's cheeks deepened in color. Drusilla's spiteful eyes shot dislike at Anabel before Ryder took her away and seated her in the supper room where she drank iced lemonade.

"Pay them no heed," he said. "You must develop a thicker skin."

"You were anxious for me to reveal myself," she accused.

"Are you implying that I had some base motive?"

"You should know your intentions best, my lord."

The Viscount swore softly. "Is it not possible for us to spend time together without quarreling?"

"I have no wish to argue with you. Now, my lord, I wish to go home."

"There are hours left in which to enjoy ourselves."

"I no longer contemplate finding pleasure in your company!"

"Running away, Anabel?"

Their eyes clashed in an angry duel before Anabel lowered her lids and sighed. "I do not want to be at outs with you, sir. Drusilla will insure that my identity is known. You cannot have considered the effect upon your consequence to be seen squiring a woman engaged in low trade."

"Low trade be damned! Nothing could be more charming than the way you conduct your Salon."

Anabel shrugged. "People who tear characters to shreds will do so whether or not they know the facts. Besides..."

"Yes...?"

"It has now become imperative that I find another hiding place. There is little above a week to my birthday. I have enough money to keep me until then. I do not know why Drusilla has kept silent, but tonight she looked so...so evil—I know she will inform on me."

"Why does she dislike you so? You can be no threat to her, poor working woman that you are!"

Anabel's eyes met his. She felt there was a significance in the way he regarded her.

He spoke again. "Even when you are one and twenty you will not be free. There is no freedom in poverty."

She felt that there was a watchfulness about him, that he waited for some word from her. Perhaps he hoped she would ask for his help. Under what conditions might he offer it? His reputation promised that he would expect to make her his mistress in return for substantial assistance.

She could not understand him. Had he no ability to experience true affection—love? He said nothing and she felt sick disappointment followed by a wave of self-disgust. She was so mesmerized by him that she knew she would be tempted to share his embraces under any circumstances.

A footman entered the supper room and bowed low. "Her Grace desires that you return to the ballroom. She wishes to know which of the country dances the lady can perform so that she may instruct the musicians."

"That settles it," said Ryder with satisfaction. "You must remain. You cannot snub the Duchess!"

Eleven

HE WAS RIGHT. She could not be discourteous to a lady who had treated her with such forbearance and they returned to join the dancers who formed a ring for "Peppers Black."

The night became blurred in a succession of dances or sitting out with Lord Ryder or the Duchess, whose patronage prevented the impertinent questions which Anabel was sure were hanging from the lips of many guests.

When finally she fell into her bed at dawn she was too tired to think and slept heavily until Sally called her with a reminder that clients were expected.

She gowned herself in a pretty blue striped cotton gown with a deeper blue sash and pulled a confection of lace over her hair. Then she began to set out cosmetics. Her mind was racing with plans to leave her lodging as soon as it was dark and it was an effort to turn to greet her visitors with a smile.

It died as she found herself confronted by Drusilla and Lord Elliot. She looked past them, nervously expecting to see Miles or his parents.

Drusilla laughed shrilly. "Oh, I haven't given you away. I have come to reassure you."

Anabel gestured toward a silk-covered couch and Drusilla sank upon it, spreading the skirts of her pink muslin gown and maroon cape. Her hair was piled in curls and decorated with maroon feathers. Her sojourn in the city did not seem to have taught her anything about dress wisdom, reflected Anabel, trying not to stare at the overapplication of rouge upon an already fiery complexion.

Elliot asked silkily, "Do not you find Drusilla's consideration admirable, Miss Hyde?"

Anabel turned her eyes to his scarlet finery, his high red heels and curled and pomaded hair, and the memory of Ryder's austere elegance flashed through her mind.

Elliot's thin mouth twisted. "You have an expressive face. Pray, cease to look at me as if I were a nature specimen or I may feel forced to disregard Drusilla's inclination and inform your relatives where you are. One might think it a duty."

Anabel afforded him a small curtsey. "I did not mean to be rude, sir."

"I am glad to know it." He took a small jewelled comfit box from his pocket and slipped a sweet into his mouth. "My throat is as dry as a sack of bran. The Duchess's wine left something to be desired."

Anabel bit back a retort that the fault most likely lay in his imbibing too freely. These two held her liberty at ransom.

"As I said," continued Drusilla, "I have not told anyone where you are. Miles has returned to Harcourt Manor, to his great annoyance, and Papa is still laid low by his gout which came the day you

184

went away. He added it to your other crimes, though for my part," she finished carelessly, "I think it was his usual bad temper and overindulgence in food and wine." She gave a smirk of satisfaction. "I received an invitation to stay with one of Mama's friends."

"Why should you care to protect me?" asked Anabel.

Her unspoken suspicion lay between them. They both knew that if Miles could marry her and secure her fortune it would increase Drusilla's chance of making an advantageous match.

Drusilla smiled. "Why should Miles have things his own way? He was beastly to me during our childhood. No, you may enjoy your freedom, Anabel, but do not annoy me, or Lord Elliot. Ain't I right, my lord?" She giggled, digging his lordship with her elbow.

Drusilla could not see the flicker of revulsion in Elliot's eyes, but he smiled with terrifying benevolence as he agreed, "Your cousin speaks truth, Miss Hyde."

The strong reek of scent was no greater than the odor of venom with which they permeated the room and after they left Anabel wondered why she should trust them. She could not and it hardened her determination to wait only for the concealing darkness to flee. She was no longer ignorant of the ways of town life and was sure she could evade the clutches of Mother Eve and her kind.

She kept a smile on her lips and a tongue full of chatter for her next clients. There was talk of the Duchess's ball and the masked lady, but it was mostly innocuous, and if speculative glances came her way they seemed good-humored.

The Salon was full when Sally admitted the Duchess of Stowebridge, who stood poised just inside the door, her fine-boned elderly hands holding a bejewelled, ribboned cane. Her hat of magnificent size boasted a large ostrich plume and her bottle-green velvet cape almost swept the floor. Anabel conducted her to a comfortable seat which had been instantly vacated by a young dandy. Then her Grace set about emptying the room by the effective expedient of glaring at anyone who dallied a second more than necessary.

Anabel poured tea from one of her pretty china teapots. The Duchess sipped, before laying her cup down. "You are well settled here, are you not, Miss Hyde?"

"I find my rooms most comfortable."

"I doubt it!" Plucked brows were drawn together in a frown. "You are not accustomed to such a dwelling."

It was a statement and Anabel could only stare as her Grace continued, "I heard about the young woman who Ryder brought to town...."

"He did not...!"

The Duchess held up an imperious hand. "That was the rumor. Do you know that both Ryder's parents died of a putrid fever when he was very young? And that he was reared by his grandmama who was my dearest friend?"

Anabel shook her head.

"She did her best, poor soul, but he came into his vast fortune at far too early an age, and although she was my friend I could see she was too weak in her love to be as strict as was necessary. She has been dead these many years, but I say nothing to you I have not said many times to her. When she saw how wild her grandson had become it was too late. He was under the influence of a rackety set of men and women. He was seduced into every kind of evil way."

The Duchess paused, her thoughts far away. "By the time he was three and twenty he had sampled every vice there was. Then he became bored. For years nothing has satisfied him. His gambling, skirt-chasing, duelling—all pursued to excess."

"Why are you telling me...?" protested Anabel. "He has been no more than a pleasing companion to me—on most occasions. He can be horrid."

The Duchess regarded her thoughtfully. "That is why I have been watching you. I have come today on behalf of both myself and my dear husband who is an invalid. We promised Ryder's grandmama on her deathbed that we would do our utmost to insure that Ryder never disgraced his antecedents by wedding an ill-bred woman." She ignored Anabel's exclamation. "He must marry. It is his duty. He argues against it, saying that no woman is chaste."

"If that is not typical! He is loose-moralled and demands a pure woman."

The Duchess was alert. "You find something in that to quarrel with?"

"Not if he seeks marriage," admitted Anabel.

"I am relieved to hear it. So you see, when I learned that Ryder was paying particular attention to a girl who seemed not to fit any of his previous notions of a mistress I became vastly curious."

She smiled gently, disregarding Anabel's indignant look. "Surely you cannot have supposed that someone of my rank would visit you here for treatment. I should have sent for you had I truly desired your help."

Anabel bit her lip and remained silent as the Duchess went on: "I was amazed that instead of some clever lightskirt I found a lady. One of more animation than beauty, of grace and charm instead of cheap wit and simpering inanities. I heard of the episode at the inn—all the town must know of it by now—and I confess I could not believe you innocent in the matter."

"Madam, I cannot allow you to think I tried to lure Ryder. The inn was a scheme devised to protect my honor. I did but ride in his carriage."

"Do not presume to raise your voice to me, miss! I believe you. Against all evidence I believe you. I think I read you aright. Does Lord Ryder care for you?"

At Anabel's wide-eyed stare the Duchess banged her cane on the floor. "Does he have a penchant for you? Does he look upon you as a true partner? In short, miss, is there a plan afoot to wed you?"

Anabel felt suddenly giddy and sat down. Ever since she had met Ryder she had been fighting the questions and answers which sought to invade her mind. Now the Duchess had brought them abruptly to her consciousness and she could not endure the knowledge thrust upon her. She loved Lord Ryder, and his ambivalent attitude toward her was searing her heart. He had kissed her with both ferocity and tenderness. He treated her with gentleness and sardonic cruelty.

The Duchess awaited a reply and Anabel stammered, "I...I do not think he has any intention of allying himself with me, ma'am."

"Suppose you are mistook—would such a match be suitable?"

"How should I know?" Anabel was sharp. She would not be examined like a beast in the marketplace, especially on behalf of a man who seemed to have lost the art of sincere emotion.

"Spare me your spurious bewilderment, miss! You know damned well what I mean! In spite of your circumstances I would swear you are a lady of quality, yet some who are born to humble parents have infiltrated the highest ranks of society. I would not care to see it in Ryder's family. Which kind are you?"

Anabel stared into the Duchess's eyes and saw an unexpected compassion, which brought her close to tears. "I am of an old and well-established family, ma'am. Hyde is not my true name."

"As I thought. What is your name?"

Anabel shook her head and the Duchess exclaimed, "Why do you live in these circumstances? Have you no money?"

Anabel said quickly, "Not very much. I pawned my possessions."

"You are willfully obtuse! I care nothing for present arrangements. Have you a fortune somewhere?"

Anabel compressed her mouth, then said, "Does

it signify? The noble Viscount has a great deal of wealth. If, by some remote chance, he should offer for me, and if," she continued, obstructing the Duchess's attempt to interrupt, "*if* I should accept him, he would have no need of more money."

"Do not pretend to be stupid! In this harsh world one can never have too much. The larger the estates the greater the protection for the family. Ryder knows that."

Anabel felt a sudden powerful need to confide in the indomitable old lady. Yet she could not. The Duchess would tell Ryder anything she felt good for him, more especially if she thought such knowledge would tip the scale in favor of a respectable alliance. Anabel wanted the Viscount with every instinct, but without the lure of anything save her person. After a lifetime of being regarded simply as the possessor of a fortune she craved the security of pure love.

"Please do not demand answers," she begged.

"You will satisfy me. Now!" ordered her Grace, banging her stick again.

Anabel's temper rose to match and she sprang to her feet. "I will not! I will keep my own counsel!"

Her Grace rose and without another word stalked to the door and threw it open, calling for her footman.

Anabel sank down, her heart thumping, her knees shaky, wondering if she had wrecked any chance in society forever. A moment later, Ryder entered, his face a mixture of surprise and amusement.

"My dear Anabel, what have you done to the

Duchess? She has just climbed into her coach and told me I would go to perdition in my own way. Then she screamed orders to her coachman and I had to leap back to avoid being run down."

"I refused to answer her questions," said Anabel.

Ryder grinned. "I wager it is the first time anyone has defied her."

"It may seem funny to you, sir, but I am apprehensive. She seemed to be my only friend in society."

"That is too unkind! What of me?"

Anabel regarded him steadily. "I suppose I must accept you to be a friend."

"So cool! I came to ask you to ride with me in Hyde Park. The day is fine, the hour is right. Say you will come."

"What a ridiculous idea!" Anabel tried to control the singing of her heart. "I have no horse, no suitable gear."

"I have brought a riding dress belonging to one of my many cousins, who was about your size, and a delightful little mare is outside. I take it you can ride."

"Yes, I enjoy it very much, but I cannot take clothes from you."

The Viscount snapped his fingers and a servant entered bearing a parcel which Ryder handed to Anabel. "Hurry and put these on. We would not wish to be late for the daily parade."

Anabel hesitated. The idea of cantering beneath trees greening with the onset of spring filled her with nostalgic longing. Riding had been one of her joys, though her mounts had been poor, and the thought of breathing fresh, daytime air was compelling.

"I deserve a reward," persuaded his lordship. "Do you recall speaking of a nursemaid who was dismissed for showing you kindness? I believe I may have traced her to a very poor part of London. My agent has still to contact her. Would you care to renew her acquaintance?"

Anabel was flustered. She had wondered what happened to the maid sent off without a character. Her prospects must have been grim. The Viscount did indeed deserve her consideration, and there was the beckoning lure of the open parkland. Most wonderful of all was the knowledge that he wanted to accompany her to a public place. Her secret exhilaration blanked out caution.

"You are exceedingly thoughtful, my lord," she murmured, picking up the parcel and hurrying to her bedchamber.

The gown fitted well and the boots were only a little too large. She smoothed down the midnight-blue cloth of the riding habit, threw the long skirt over her arm and returned to Ryder, who gave her an appreciative survey before handing her a wide-brimmed hat of the same blue, trimmed with ribbon and a silver buckle, and a crop and leather gloves.

Anabel frowned. They looked suspiciously new. Ryder smiled. "I swear they all came from my cousin. She has grown too plump for the dress since she bore her second child and she is notoriously lazy. She has seldom used the things."

Anabel tried on the hat, finding it impossible

not to be glad that Sally had persuaded her to change her severe coiffure. The maid had been busy with scissors and curling tongs and Anabel's hair was drawn into a smooth chignon, leaving small curls to fall over her ears and forehead.

She was pleased with her appearance and turned to precede Ryder from the room when she realized he was holding a final item. A black velvet mask.

Her pleasure died. She could not put out her hand and Ryder said, "I have to confess that I purchased this. You will wish to wear it, will you not?"

She stared at him. He was using her for his amusement. Had the whole outing been planned as a charade?

He spoke again. "I have assumed that you intend to maintain your ruse by masking yourself in public. *La belle masquée*, as the Duchess has it."

Had he no notion that she had imagined for a brief, joyful time that he wanted to be seen with her? She had even been prepared to risk recognition in her exultation. What a fool she was! She could not find words to argue with him. She might reveal her innermost feelings. She removed the hat and Ryder tied the strings of the mask behind her head. The soft movements of his fingers on her hair sent tremors of longing through her. She jerked the hat back on and they descended the stairs.

The mare was an exquisite creature. The sun shone warmly and the breeze was scented with the promise of summer. The grass was soft and sweet smelling beneath the horses' hooves, but Anabel could not recapture her pleasure. She countered the stares of other riders with cool looks and spoke as little as possible, urging her mount into a gallop whenever she thought the Viscount was about to become serious.

By the time he returned her to her rooms he looked furious. With justification, Anabel admitted. His bringing the mask was logical and sensible, but she had wanted none of his logic and sense today. She had ached for a brief hour of freedom and had been prepared to be reckless to obtain it. She found the Viscount incomprehensible. At the Masquerade she was sure he had desired her to remove her mask. Yet today he had gone to the trouble of purchasing a new one. She gave him no time to speak but hurried away to remove the borrowed garments which she sent to him by Sally, saying she had the headache and would remain in her room.

When she peeped through the curtains and saw him ride away she knew an irrational disappointment. Why did he not force her to break her barrier of silence? She longed to engage in a battle of words. Her mind and body yearned for contact with his and she felt shame for her wanton weakness.

She waited impatiently for the onset of darkness when it would be easier for her to leave undetected. What would Ryder do when he found her gone? She would not even tell Sally. He would understand one day, if he cared enough to ask.

Doubts kept assailing her. Her love for Ryder, released by the Duchess's searching questions, was growing by the hour. It was being borne in upon her that pride should be sacrificed to love. Once her Grace knew the truth Anabel had no doubt she would find sanctuary in Grosvenor Square. At last she admitted to herself that to leave her lodging to seek another refuge, alone, would be an act of folly. She might not be lucky a second time.

She was at her table, drawing writing materials and quill toward her when a messenger brought a letter in Ryder's hand. She tore it open. "Madam," she read, and a smile quirked the corners of her mouth. He was still indignant! The letter continued: "Your nurse-girl from your past has been traced and is in dire need. She is destitute and gravely ill, and without help will surely perish. I will send my carriage for you in half an hour. Pray, be ready to accompany me to her lodging, if you so desire."

Anabel glanced at the messenger in Ryder's livery. "I will be ready," she said quietly, and he left.

She must forget her need in the deeper one of the woman who had given her some hope during her childhood, and she scribbled a note for Sally, who was out marketing.

Within twenty minutes she was stepping into a town carriage. The groom put up the steps and she turned to greet Lord Ryder who was lounging in the corner, his chin sunk into his collar, a wide-brimmed beaver hat pulled forward so that his face was in shadow.

So he was still sulking, but she owed him gratitude for his consideration in finding the hapless maid, and she murmured her thanks.

He shrugged wordlessly and she turned from

him. He should not have the chance of snubbing her further.

She leaned back, looking out at the bustle of laundrymaids and street hawkers, tattered beggars and sedan chairs bearing some fine lady or gentleman to an evening rendezvous.

Once or twice she gave a sidelong glance at the motionless, quiet figure in the other corner of the coach, marveling at the anomaly of a man who would not break a sullen silence even while he could not turn aside from duty to an old servant in need. She supposed she loved him in spite of his inconsistencies—or perhaps because of them.

The aristocratic streets were giving way to narrow, evil-smelling places, where doors opened onto the slimy cobbles and ragged children played dangerously near the horses' hooves.

Anabel thought of the nurse whom she recalled as plump and rosy-cheeked, smelling of lavender, and she shuddered to think how such a girl had been brought to these conditions.

Now the carriage was in streets so narrow that it seemed the horse would not be able to draw it between the half-derelict houses.

Anabel turned to Ryder in horror. "What is this place called, my lord?"

The world turned to a waking nightmare as the man straightened his shoulders and lifted his hat.

She was sharing a coach with Lord Elliot.

In a crazy impulse she tried to open her door and he restrained her with a vicious grip, "Do you want to kill yourself?"

"Death would be preferable to you!"

"How quickly you fell for my ruse," remarked his lordship casually.

"The messenger was in Ryder's livery; the crest on the coach door was his," she protested, unable to accept the awful situation. "The note was in his hand! You are teasing me, are you not?"

"Do go on," begged Elliot. "The game is more amusing than I had hoped."

Anabel was jerked back in her seat as the horses quickened pace on a stretch of open road. "Where are we going?"

"You will find out in good time."

Anabel ground her knuckles on her teeth. Was she victim of some vengeful scheme in which Ryder was implicated? She felt she could not live with such abhorrent suspicion.

Hope tugged at her as she felt the horses slowing at the first toll. She leaned forward, ready to make a desperate bid for freedom. Immediately Elliot was pinning her arms to her side, pulling her close. The footman had the necessary coins ready to hand, and as they rolled through the toll Elliot sank his mouth on hers in a sickening kiss.

He released her almost at once and watched with a twisted smile as she scrubbed at her mouth with her handkerchief.

"Do not fear for your virtue, madam. If you wish to remain unmolested you had best behave at the tolls. I shall not touch you unless you make it necessary."

Anabel felt close to despair. She asked again

197

where they were heading, but he ignored her. She could not endure the idea of his mouth on hers and they passed the remaining tolls without incident.

On a lonely stretch of road they stopped to transfer to a traveling coach and fear enveloped her again. She began to think. They must pause somewhere if only to change horses. Surely there would be a chance for her to get away. Traffic grew lighter as they covered the miles until they met only an occasional stage, a fast-moving mail coach, or parties of open carriages filled with laughing men and girls returning to their country homes from some exploratory trip.

To Anabel's despair they did not stop for a change of horse and must have covered thirty miles. The sky had deepened to dark blue by the time they pulled to a halt.

Anabel's hope that she might enlist aid died as she stared through the window. The building before which they had stopped was mean and ill kept. A swinging sign with paintwork half-obliterated proclaimed it to be an inn, but she could not expect to find anyone respectable here.

When the coach door was opened she descended the steps and her cramped legs caused her almost to fall on to the cracked paving stones of the inn yard.

A hand was put out to save her and she looked up into the grinning face of her cousin, Miles Bulmore.

Twelve

BEYOND MILES STOOD DRUSILLA, her face equally triumphant, her eyes coquettish as she greeted Lord Elliot. In panic Anabel turned to run, but the men caught her easily and held her tight between them. She was hustled past the sweating horses, their heads hanging, into the inn, where a grimy parlor awaited them.

Elliot said in disgust, "Is this the best you could do? My throat is cracking for want of a drink, but I cannot believe there is anything fit here—or clean either," he added, dusting a chair with a lace handkerchief, before seating himself.

"Now don't be hasty," admonished Drusilla, in coyly chiding tones. "I took the precaution of bringing bottles and glasses with me."

"Clever!" said Elliot.

His emphasis might have been construed by anyone more perceptive than Drusilla as satirical, but she was engaged in pouring a glass of brandy which she handed to Lord Elliot.

"There you are, my lord. See how I am already learning your tastes."

Anabel swayed, feeling the color drain from her face as she stared into Miles's malignant eyes. He put out a fleshy hand and touched her arm. She jerked herself away and his plump cheeks reddened. "Play the fine lady while you can. My turn will come."

"What do you mean?"

"You imagine you have been so clever, don't you? Do you really think my sister such a ninny as to let a prize pigeon like you slip away. We have been in tucks over your antics. You are very gullible."

Anabel's lip curled. "Indeed! And does that include all of you?"

Elliot refilled his glass and grinned at the others. "She means to ask if that includes Ryder, is not that so, my dear Miss Hyde—Harcourt, I should say?"

Color ran briefly beneath Anabel's ashen skin as Miles jeered, "Did you suppose that the proud Viscount Ryder was going to offer for you?"

Elliot snapped, "Enough! You have trapped your quarry! Administer the kill and let us finish the hunt."

Anabel's eyes widened and Drusilla laughed, "You must not take my lord so seriously. We shall not harm you. In fact, Miles is going to cherish and comfort you for the rest of your life."

"True," said Miles. "You were very naughty to try to escape us. Your guardians have always known what is best for you."

"Marriage to you!" gasped Anabel, repugnance in her face and voice.

Miles was petulant. "I do not know how I shall

manage her! I always knew she was not so nice in her notions as she made out."

Elliot exclaimed in disgust. "You can wed her and get her with child, I suppose. That will keep her quiet. Then you can leave her in the country and enjoy her fortune in town."

"*After* you have made over my share to me—and my husband," reminded Drusilla, placing a proprietary hand on Elliot's shoulder.

Anabel's eyes blazed contempt.

"Ryder could have saved you," remarked Drusilla, "if he had not spurned me at Vauxhall. After that we could not allow you to take your fortune from us."

"You have made things difficult," complained Miles. "Always in your rooms or with Ryder, but we caught you in the end. Elliot told us what to do."

"I do not doubt it," said Anabel.

Elliot's voice was silky. "It was a good plan, was it not? How easily you fell for the sight of blue and gold livery. And am I not expert at producing my cousin's writing?"

"So Ryder did not conspire with you!"

Anabel could not keep relief from her voice and Elliot's knuckles whitened.

"Enough," snapped Drusilla. She brought a chair to Anabel. "Sit down!"

Anabel hesitated, then sank down, holding her hands tightly together to control their tremor. Miles produced a glass of wine which Drusilla handed to Anabel.

"Get this down you, and hurry. We still have a long way to travel."

"Where are you taking me?"

"To your rightful home, of course," put in Miles. "There you will find a welcome and there you will remain until our wedding day, three days from now. The county is quite intrigued by the whole affair."

Hope flickered in the depths of Anabel's horror. Had they announced the wedding openly? Could they truly think that she would meekly wed Miles with the whole world and his wife looking on? She would cry aloud that she was being shamefully misused and forced into a hateful union.

Drusilla said, correctly interpreting her thoughts, "We have told everyone that you have been exceedingly ill. That is why our neighbors were not surprised at your long confinement in your bedchamber. Of course, Mama, with Tabitha's help, has allowed no one but herself to tend you. She has been much admired for her devotion. You would have been amazed had you witnessed the general concern when the physician told of your dreadful weakness and your courage in—"

"What physician? Our family medical man would never connive in so wicked a fashion!"

"Him! We did not call him! No, we sent for a man from London. Folk were much impressed," interrupted Miles. "We laughed ourselves silly afterwards to think how the county was taken in by an actor."

Anabel stared at her three tormentors. She

could not conceive how they thought to succeed in their plan.

Drusilla pushed the filled glass into her hand. "Drink," she ordered.

Anabel lifted her eyes to her cousin's and what she read there made her dash the glass aside. The wine spilled down the front of Drusilla's bright yellow gown. She stared at it, then went to a table where she poured another glass of wine which she brought back.

Standing just out of Anabel's reach she said, "Yes, the wine is drugged. As you will be until you are assisted down the aisle by your uncle. Everyone knows how you have implored us to allow the wedding plans to go forward so that even if you die you will have the joy of being tied to the man you love. I am told by Mama that several ladies wept openly."

"Why do you not drink, Miss Harcourt?" suggested Elliot. "You will in the end, you know."

"I shall not move an inch to help you in your filthy scheme," grated Anabel.

Elliot sighed, rose, and joined Miles and Drusilla as they stood over Anabel. "I make my apologies in advance, ma'am," he said, "but a man must live. My debts are heavy and debtors are pressing."

He seized her arms and Miles held her legs. Drusilla jerked her head back by her hair and, as Anabel opened her mouth in a gasp of pain, poured wine down her throat. She choked and coughed as the bitter liquid filled her mouth. She spat it out,

203

but Drusilla kept pouring until Anabel felt her senses swimming.

"What . . . what . . . ?" she articulated, her tongue thick and sluggish.

"Laudanum," said Drusilla. "Harmless enough, though you must not force us to give you too much."

Her smiling face wavered before Anabel's eyes. She struggled to focus, but Miles and Elliot seemed to be floating in mist. As through a blanket she heard Elliot say, "I hope to God you know what you are doing, Drusilla. We do not want her dead."

Anabel tried to speak, but her tongue was paralyzed. She felt herself lifted and carried to the coach. She heard the shouts of ostlers, the stamp of horses, the movement of the carriage. She could not sit unsupported and knew that Miles and Lord Elliot were taking turns to hold her upright. She cringed inwardly from the feel of their arms about her, but she was helpless.

Then her mind began to play cruel tricks. She was in a boat; she was with Ryder and he loved her. He was embracing her and she tried to turn to him to tell him that she returned his love. Elliot spoke and the dream was shattered. The miles passed and she wavered between sleep and half-realized wakefulness, unable to separate reality from illusion.

She felt sick. Something about her mumbles alerted the others, for they stopped at a wayside cottage and a bowl and linens were brought. Then, exhausted beyond measure, Anabel slept in truth.

Once, when the fog in her brain began to clear, Drusilla poured more wine into her and again she drifted into fantasy. She knew they were at Harcourt Manor when she heard the thin tones of her uncle.

"So you have her! Quickly, the servants are at their meal. Hurry!"

Anabel was carried upstairs.

"Are you sure no one knows where she is?" That was her aunt.

"Positive, ma'am!" The languid voice of Lord Elliot. "She did not know where she was bound herself. She thought she was going to another part of London."

"Excellent!"

Anabel was undressed by her aunt and Tabitha and left in bed. She sensed that the maid was sitting near her, watching. She tried to fight the thick darkness, but waves of nausea overtook her and she closed her eyes and floated from misery into oblivion.

She awoke at dawn, puzzled by the different direction of the light through the window. Abruptly she recalled what had happened and tried to sit up. Everything shimmered and swayed in sickening movement and she fell back. Her mouth was kiln-dry. A jug and a glass were on her bedside table, but she could not reach them. A low moan escaped her.

There was a scraping of a chair and Tabitha stood, hands on hips, glaring at her. "So you're awake! A fine dance you've led us! All night I've been out of my bed watching over you. What you've got against Master Miles I'll never know."

Anabel gestured to the water and Tabitha's eyes narrowed. "Thirsty? Uncomfortable? Well, it's nothing to what you'll be if you try to run away again."

She permitted Anabel a small measure of water and she drank avidly, then sank back. "How... how can you...connive in such...wickedness?" she managed.

The maid frowned. "I know my place, as you ought to know yours. You ought to show gratitude for the way your uncle and aunt have reared you."

Words of bitter rejection screamed in Anabel's head, but her lids closed and she drifted into sleep. She lost track of light and dark. The wedding day must be almost upon her. She could not resist the drugged slops which were poured into her. They had decreased the dosage of laudanum and she supposed they meant her to walk, supported, to the altar and articulate something. She would make someone in the church aware of her anguish—she would!

Drusilla came to see her. "The wedding is to be entirely private in deference to your illness, Anabel."

Anabel groaned. The ancient, half-blind priest would detect nothing. The Bulmores would have it their own way. Thoughts of Miles and his pudgy face and hands, his nauseous embraces, sent shudders through her weakened frame and tears sliding down her cheeks.

Her aunt wiped them away, talking briskly. "If you had a spark of consideration for your own father's sister none of this would have been necessary. It was your absolute duty to keep your fortune in the family. You know how straightened are our circumstances."

"Please, Aunt . . . I will be generous. . . . I always meant to...you may have all my wealth if you will release me...."

She thought she caught a flicker of uncertainty and hope flared, then died as her aunt said, "It is too late, even if I trusted you! You have always been so secretive. I never could comprehend you! The marriage has been arranged and will take place."

"When?"

"Tomorrow. Your gown is ready. There will be a small reception here afterwards for our neighbors who will understand that you are unable to join the festivities, but I shall be sure to allow a sight of the marriage lines to the ladies. This will be no hole-in-the-corner affair to give rise to speculation."

They helped Anabel out of bed and dressed her in white. She felt the softness of silk and muslin and lace. Her sacrificial garments would be the finest the Bulmores had ever allowed her. They placed a white hat trimmed with small silver roses on her head.

When they led her to a cheval glass she saw that she wore a gleaming pearl necklace and ear-drops, and out of the past came a memory of her mother wearing the jewels. Her face was as white as her garments, her eyes deep-shadowed, the pupils contracted.

They would have no difficulty in convincing any onlookers that she was extremely ill. She knew by her failing senses that she had been drugged again. Her whole spirit was trying to voice itself in protest, but her body would not obey. Within an hour she would be irrevocably tied to a man who filled her with hatred and disgust.

Farmhands and villagers shouted goodwill messages as the carriage rolled by.

"They have been given the morning off and are to have a splendid feast tonight," said Anabel's uncle.

Anabel stared out at them, envying their freedom to choose their mates. She would have traded all she owned for an equal opportunity. The resignation of despair was destroying her will as the carriage stopped at the church lych-gate and the steps were lowered. Drusilla was waiting, gowned in pale blue. Anabel gathered the remnants of her strength to avoid the urging of her uncle's hands, but she found herself standing by Drusilla, clinging to a posy of flowers which had been shoved at her, listening to murmurs of sympathy from village women who stood at a respectful distance.

Then, supported on each side, she was turned toward the gate. She stumbled and almost fell, and the pounding of her heart began to beat a crescendo in her ears. Her uncle held her in a viciously tight grasp and Drusilla tugged at her.

Her heartbeats grew louder and she felt her uncle stiffen as he looked over his shoulder. He began to drag her toward the gate and Anabel realized that the pounding was partly of horses' hooves. The riders were dangerously near, and her uncle and Drusilla released their hold and sprang back to safety. Anabel closed her eyes. She would be trampled and she did not care. Death would be welcome.

She was caught by her slender waist and lifted to a saddle. Steel-strong arms were about her and the galloping motion of a horse was beneath her.

A voice she knew laughed aloud. "In the nick of time, Anabel! In the nick of time!"

Anabel sagged against Lord Ryder, relief almost unseating her, but he held her secure, and listening to the shouts and screams of fury receding into the distance she gave herself up to the wonder and joy of knowing that she was held safe by the man she loved.

There were other riders. He had brought assistants with him. How had he known where to find her? Questions surfaced and sank as she lay back against him, reveling in the strength of his heartbeats, the power in his hands over the great animal they rode.

They traveled across fields and along byways where no coach could follow and stopped at a small hunting lodge. Anabel was helped from the horse and Ryder carried her into the house and up a shining oak stairway. He laid her gently on a half-tester bed and left her to the ministrations of two maids in print aprons and mob caps. They clucked their sympathy at her helpless condition. Tears slid from beneath her lids, but as she attempted to explain that they were tears of happiness, sleep claimed her.

She was watched over constantly by the maids as days and nights slipped by. Ryder came often to visit her and one morning she was able to conquer the drug-induced weakness and walk in the garden, leaning on his arm, breathing the mingled scents of spring.

They rested on a bench beneath an archway of clematis. Ryder wore boots and breeches, a dark country coat and plain shirt. A stock was loosely knotted round his strong throat.

"I have been deeply anxious about you, Anabel. Had it not been that the scandal would involve your blood relatives I would have given them in charge for so monstrously dangerous an attack."

"Oh, my lord..." The foolish tears stung the backs of her eyes. "I am sorry—of late I keep weeping—it is all so silly."

Ryder's mouth tightened. "Not so, my dear, after your suffering!"

"How did you find me?"

"Sally found a letter purporting to come from me. Knowing your great fear of your family I immediately thought of them, and when I discovered that Drusilla had gone hastily out of town I decided to make for Harcourt Manor."

He looked momentarily vulnerable. "I did not realize you were missing until it was almost too late. We were on our way to the manor when I saw you at the church gate."

She held her breath and waited, hoping, half expecting him to make some kind of declaration. He did not and disappointment gave her a flash of her old retaliation. "If you had arrived but a quarter of an hour later! Were you still—sulking, my lord?"

"Always imputing the finest of motives to me!

I was not—sulking, as you put it. I have tracked down your former nurse-girl...."

"But that was a trick! Elliot said..."

"Not so, Anabel. My kinsman is clever. He knows that a mix of truth and deceit is infallible. I really have tracked your maid. My dear cousin must have a spy in my household. Make no mistake, the creature will be apprehended and dealt with. The same misbegotten servant stole a suit of livery. Your maid was in great need. She was so ill I sent at once for my own physician. I engaged nurses for she could not be moved. I spent quite a lot of time in her vile hovel. I wanted to restore her to you."

"Oh, how good of you! Poor creature! Is she...?"

"She is recovering. She is installed in a much better dwelling where you may visit her."

"What an act of charity, my lord. I had not thought..." She stopped, realizing that her sentiment of surprise at his benevolence was scarcely flattering.

Ryder grinned. "You need not dissemble, Anabel. I have not been famous for eccentric liberality."

"Why did you help her?"

He shrugged, looking, for a moment, discomfited. "Call it a whim."

Anabel looked down at her hands. "Did...did she talk much to you? Perhaps of my childhood?"

She looked up quickly and caught a glint at the back of his eyes. "Do you know, Anabel, that there are times when your looks surpass beauty."

She was assailed by a mingling of disappointment and hope. When he took one of her hands her heart jumped erratically. But he only bent his

211

dark head to kiss her fingertips. "Tomorrow we return to London."

Ryder had sent for his most comfortable traveling coach and by leaving at dawn they reached the capital late the same day. Anabel had dozed and was surprised to discover that they had not halted in Bond Street.

"This is Grosvenor Square—her Grace's residence!"

"Where you will be an honored guest." Ryder bowed, helping her out of the coach and leading her into the hall, where the Duchess came to greet her.

"At last! I could scarce believe it when Ryder wrote me. How dare your relatives use you so disgracefully. You must stay with me until your strength is fully returned."

"Thank you, your Grace. You are most kind."

"Nonsense! It is high time some lady took you in hand. And as for you, Ryder, you can take yourself off and get into some decent town gear before you call again."

Lord Ryder grinned and left, and Anabel allowed herself to be conducted to a bedchamber where she sank on to a soft daybed before a glowing coal fire.

"And now," said the Duchess, seating herself firmly upon a chair on the other side of the fireplace, "you will tell me exactly why you have been playing your charade and why your wicked aunt and uncle were so anxious to marry you to your cousin."

She expressed no amazement when she learned of Anabel's fortune. "There was bound to be money in it. Your man of business will be asked to make you a full account, of course. He has neglected your interests shamefully."

Anabel concluded, "I have safely passed my birthday, though I fear I shall be forced to lean on country society for amusement. The *ton* world will reject me for having engaged in trade."

Her Grace did not trouble to hide the gaps in her teeth in a malevolent grin. "Do not worry. You will be astonished to discover how many of the *haut ton* will consider your activities only the amusing eccentricities of a privileged lady when they learn how rich you are. *I* will chaperon you. And Ryder will, in any case, make your way easy."

Anabel did not reply. She believed that his lordship's concern, his romantic ride, were engendered mainly by his refusal to allow anyone, especially Drusilla and Lord Elliot, to get the better of him.

She opened her eyes on the following day to discover that Sally had arrived and she was assisted into a gown of pale pink sprigged muslin and a lacy white shawl. Her hair was dressed in the becoming style of chignon and tiny curls.

The Duke and Duchess were still abed when Ryder called. He was ushered into Anabel's presence in the pretty morning room. His elegant town garb looked as if it had been tailored around him, his cravat tied to perfection and secured with a single diamond pin, but Anabel felt a stab of nostalgia for his country clothes.

She expressed her relief that no action had been instigated against her relatives. "I will not have them punished," she said. "My aunt is still Papa's sister."

"As you will."

There was a brief silence and Anabel said, "Her Grace is of the opinion that I shall be accepted into society in spite of the beauty venture."

"I am glad to hear it."

Anabel stared at him. Suddenly she no longer cared about society. It held no attraction for her without Ryder to share it. And it seemed that his past existence had rendered it impossible for him to surrender his heart.

She was so lost in dismal reflection that it surprised her to realize he was taking her hands in his. "You will be utterly safe from now on—in my protection."

"I do not require your patronage, sir."

"Patronage be damned! I am asking you to marry me."

Bliss melted her bones, but she could not easily relinquish her suspicions. "Why?"

His answer was to slide his arms about her and take the lips she lifted irresistibly.

"I love you," he murmured against her mouth. "When I knew you were in danger I could not endure the agony."

Joy invaded her as his lips explored her face. "Lovely, sweetest of women. You call forth all that is best in me. If Miles Bulmore had violated you I would have killed him."

Together they sat upon a brocaded couch and Ryder held her close to his side. "I must learn a new language, my darling. The language of true love. You know I have had a most doubtful past, but I have never loved before. I have never even understood the meaning of love."

He stroked her hair and his hands sent shivers of longing through her. "How courageous you are! When I saw you about to step into that dreadful basket on the stagecoach I was utterly confounded."

"I was thankful you stopped me," admitted Anabel. "Ryder, why did you not confess your love for me at the hunting lodge? I have been in such doubt."

"Did you imagine I would make love to you, unchaperoned as you were?"

"You kissed me when I was alone in a bedchamber at an inn."

"That was different."

"It certainly was. You forced yourself upon me."

His voice grew a little haughty. "That was not what I meant. You can surely understand that a man may kiss a woman he scarcely knows without the dangers attendant upon an embrace for the woman he adores. I have not been used to continence, madam, and I was joyful and relieved that you were safe."

"Oh!" Color flooded Anabel's cheeks. "Let us not quarrel. I have waited so long—hoped so much...."

The Duchess was full of delightful plans. "I shall stand in lieu of a mother to you, Anabel. The Duke and I have decided that you must be wed from here."

Happy days were passed in contemplation of fashion plates and swatches of material sent from every reputable warehouse. Modistes and milliners, jewellers and shoemakers fought to reach

Grosvenor Square first when the news was leaked that her Grace of Stowebridge was sponsoring the wedding of an heiress and a Viscount.

Then, in a stroke, Anabel's joy was desecrated. A letter from Drusilla, blotched and ill spelt, written in high fury said, "I am told that Ryder has offered for you. You pretend to want love but you are quick to grab a title. I suppose he is to recoup his lost fortune with yours. Everyone knows that gambling on horses, cards and 'Change have done for him. Everyone knows also that the Duchess will do anything to help him. I wish you joy of your match!"

Anabel screwed up the letter, then spread it out and read it again. Ryder had admitted his heavy gambling. And the Duchess had been deeply inquisitive about her finances. But there were others with larger fortunes than hers! And with guardians to see that they did not marry rakehells, whispered a voice from within. Her precarious confidence in herself was shattered. She could not help loving Ryder, but she must know the truth. She doubted that she could sufficiently demean herself to wed a man who used her for her money, however much she cared.

In the evening he called and they sat in the library. The fire drew gleams from his hair and lit sparks in his eyes.

"Do...do you truly love me, my lord?" she asked.

She could not deceive him. He looked searchingly at her as he answered with a question. "Why do you ask? And in such a way?"

"A woman needs constant reassurance."

"You are no ordinary woman. Do not play co-quette!"

"What game do you play with me?"

"What in hell's got into you?"

"Do you know the extent of my fortune, sir?"

Ryder's brows went up. "I do."

"When did you learn of it?"

"Your nurse-girl was eager to talk to me."

"I see. And that was the first you knew?"

He rose, walked to the fireplace and kicked a log into the heart of the flames. A shower of sparks shot up as he turned to face her. "No! I made inquiries some while ago."

Anabel could taste her disappointment. "Have you lost a fortune gambling, my lord?"

Ryder looked curiously at her. "A veritable fortune, my dear. I have never disciplined myself. Have I pretended otherwise?"

"My money will be useful to you."

"To us, my dear."

Anabel's voice was low. "Why could you not have been honest? Oh, you have not lied in words, but in your silence. God help me, I think I would still have wanted you whatever the circumstances, but you could not trust me, could you? If only you could understand how I long to be loved in truth. But you are not capable..."

She could not bear to look at him again. She turned and ran from the room, up to her bedchamber, where she locked the door and paced the room in anguish too deep for tears.

The Duchess received the news that the wedding was off with disbelief. "Have you run mad? You are the first woman he has cared for."

"He has not the capacity to care for anyone but himself."

The Duchess controlled her tongue with difficulty. "A lovers' tiff. It will blow over."

"It will not."

The Duchess glared into Anabel's stubborn face as the butler announced, "Viscount Ryder, your Grace."

Anabel greeted him with lifted chin. He answered with a cool nod.

The Duchess banged the table. "Devil take you both! What nonsense is this?"

Anabel's voice was high and toneless. "It seems, ma'am, that his lordship has known all along that I am wealthy and simply wishes to recoup his gaming losses. I want no husband on those terms."

The Duchess's mouth dropped open. "What does the girl mean?"

"I mean, ma'am, that Lord Ryder should have been honest with me."

The Duchess's astonishment deepened. "Good God! If every intending spouse was honest society would fall apart at the seams!"

The Viscount suppressed a grin as the Duchess continued, "Your wits are awandering, Anabel. Ryder's fortune gone! Who fed you such a fantasy?"

Anabel said uncertainly, "He did not deny it."

"I am not surprised if you treated him with such disdain as you are displaying now. But, then, you have had no experience with men."

"A condition I require in my bride," interposed Ryder, his voice shaking a little.

"You find me amusing, my lord?" Anabel was full of hauteur.

"Amusing! Diverting! Wonderful! Adorable!" assured Ryder. "And I forgive you freely for attributing such base behavior to me."

"Do you mean you are not ruined? That you are still rich?"

"I fear so, ma'am. Quite disgracefully possessed of wealth! I have been to my lawyer and he is ready to show you proof of my estates and their healthy revenues."

The Duchess looked astonished. "It is for the Duke to assist with marriage settlements and all that kind of thing, Ryder. Your lawyer will call on his Grace as soon as he is sent for."

She stared at Anabel. "Where can you have gleaned such odd notions? Ah! I recall now that a letter was delivered to you from Somerset."

"Do you dare tell me that you believed lies of me sent you by your false relatives?" demanded Ryder.

"I crave your pardon, my lord. But the Duchess asked me many questions about money."

Her Grace drew back her chin. "So! What of it? As it happens, my girl, Ryder told me he had fallen hopelessly in love with you soon after you arrived in London. He cared not a brass farthing for your money, or for the fact that you lived over a china shop and dealt in cosmetics. *I* wanted to take you under my protection, but he would not hear of it. Said you'd be safer hid there from your grasping relatives who had law on their side and could order your life until you reached one and twenty. It's my belief, though, that the idiot man was enjoying the play. And as for you, Anabel, I am surprised you cannot tell when a man loves you. He even got me to send you a maid I had in training and paid her proper wages."

"Sally came from you?"

Ryder's face was alight with mirth.

Anabel flared, "When we met you had a poor opinion of me! You would have put me on the stagecoach."

"Ah, but do not forget I would not allow you to suffer in the rumble-tumble."

"You dumped me in Bond Street where I was almost lured to a life of vice by a dreadful woman and her bully."

"And where Kitty Prowse rescued you."

"You sent her?"

"Naturally. I despatched a messenger from our beleaguered inn. Wicked and arrogant though I am—or rather was—I could not allow such an innocent to be accosted by such as Mother Eve."

He looked reflectively at Anabel. "Or maybe I had begun to care for you without realizing it."

"And I thought you sent the postilion on a frivolous errand."

"Well, I did write to the Duchess also. And you had no way of discerning that beneath my rakehell exterior lay a heart aching for pure love."

Anabel raised her delicate brows. "What would you have done if I had obtained no clients?"

Ryder had the grace to color a little. "Er, one

of the aspects of living a life of sinful merriment is that one unavoidably becomes acquainted with the more, er, abandoned areas of London. Naturally, I need hardly impress upon you that it is all behind me forever, and you confounded me, I confess, by becoming a beauty expert. My admiration for you has been—"

Anabel cut him short. "*You* sent Laughing Dorcas and Fighting Bet?"

"Not personally, you comprehend. Kitty arranged it. And ponder on this, Anabel, my love, I had no idea that you were rich and could only surmise that you were well born. I inquired into your background only when I was forced to admit that I loved you to distraction."

"You cannot take exception to that," stated the Duchess. "A man is entitled to know his wife's antecedents even if he chooses to ignore them."

"What would you have done had I unmasked at the ball?"

"What do you think I would have done?" he inquired gently.

"You seemed anxious for me to reveal myself."

"My dear child, I had the intention of silencing all tongues and making you safe by announcing an attachment for you. We should have been betrothed, that is, if you had consented. I think your relatives would not have presumed to interfere."

Anabel felt hot with chagrin. "I could have saved us so much!"

"You could indeed!"

"Ah, yes," she recalled, "but what about the day you handed me a mask to wear in the park?"

"So I did! You had made it absolutely clear that you wished to remain anonymous! You permitted me to tie the strings."

This was unarguable and Anabel put out her hand. "Surely you guessed I thought ill of you, Ryder. Why did you let me continue in such an error?"

Ryder paused, and for the first time since they met he looked uncertain. "I was afraid. You succeeded in introducing me to cowardice as no man or woman has ever done. I helped you at first because you were so courageous. I held you in high esteem for that. Then, I found myself wanting you and I tried to keep away from you."

Anabel looked sharply at him.

"Oh, not because I thought you unsuitable for me, my darling. I could not help loving you. But for the first time in my life I dared not test a woman's emotions toward me. Time and again I went to your rooms. So often there were others present. Sometimes I left without entering at all. And you appeared so supremely in command of your situation. You appeared to need no man's love to support you—least of all mine."

"We were alone several times, my lord."

"So we were, Anabel. And we seemed always to argue. Believe me, my dear, I have had to learn a whole new pattern of manners for your sake."

"Our quarreling was my fault too," admitted Anabel.

The Duchess emitted what might, in a lady of lesser degree, be regarded as a snort. "Is this to continue all night?"

222

She received no reply. Anabel felt life itself pulsate with renewed vigor in the light which glowed from the Viscount's eyes. Again she held out her hand and this time he took it, drew her close and kissed her gently.

"Dinner," articulated the Duchess, "should have been served a quarter of an hour ago. I dislike waiting for my food. I am going for mine."

She walked to the door and turned to survey the lovers. "I daresay you will be very happy. Actually, I think you will aggravate one another beyond endurance of any normal mortal, but you will call it love! And how you will enjoy making up your differences!"

She stalked out and Ryder held Anabel even closer.

Her Grace stuck her head round the door. "Mind! I shall expect to be guest of honor at the wedding!" She vanished again.

Lord Ryder and Anabel had scarcely heard her.

"Shall we eat, my dearest?" asked the Viscount.

Anabel nodded. "I believe I shall enjoy my food as never before, my love."

"A sentiment which will undoubtedly apply to both of us in everything we do together," pronounced his lordship in tones of deep fulfilment.

Let COVENTRY Give You
A Little Old-Fashioned Romance